'Mr Tarrant?' ... weakly.

'Julian Tarrant,' ... expect Frankie Somers, but if *he* couldn't make it there was little point in his sending his secretary.'

'*I* am Frankie Somers,' she informed him haughtily. 'It may be a man's world up the Limpopo, Mr Tarrant, but in publishing circles it's unwise to presume.'

'Good lord!' he said disgustedly. 'What the devil can they be thinking of, sending a woman editor?'

Dear Reader

What a great selection of romances we have in store for you this month—we think you'll love them! How about a story of love and passion, set in the glamorous world of the movies—with deception and double-dealing to thrill you? Or perhaps you'd prefer a romance with the added spice of revenge . . .? We can offer you all this and more! And, with exotic locations such as Egypt, Costa Rica and the South Pacific to choose from, your only problem will be deciding which of our exciting books to read first!

The Editor

Lee Stafford was born and educated in Sheffield where she worked as a secretary, and later as a public relations assistant. However, she has been a compulsive scribbler for as long as she can remember. She lives in Sussex with her husband, their two teenage daughters and three cats. To keep fit, she swims and does a weekly dance-exercise class. When not travelling to research new backgrounds, she likes to relax at the small apartment they recently bought in France.

Recent titles by the same author:

WHEN LOVE AWAKES

AN EASY MAN TO LOVE

BY

LEE STAFFORD

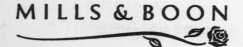

MILLS & BOON

MILLS & BOON LIMITED
ETON HOUSE, 18-24 PARADISE ROAD
RICHMOND, SURREY TW9 1SR

*MILLS & BOON and the Rose Device
are trademarks of the publisher.*

*First published in Great Britain 1994
by Mills & Boon Limited*

© Lee Stafford 1994

*Australian copyright 1994   Philippine copyright 1994
This edition 1994*

ISBN 0 263 78701 X

*Set in Times Roman 10 on 12 pt.
01-9410-53600 C*

Made and printed in Great Britain

CHAPTER ONE

IT WAS sheeting down with rain when the London train pulled into Poole station, and what would, Frankie supposed, have been a stupendous view over the vast, almost landlocked expanse of the famous harbour was blotted out and all but invisible. That had been disappointment number one, but she had reminded herself resignedly that she had never nurtured great hopes for this trip, anyhow.

If possible, the weather had worsened as the bus laboured and droned along the country roads through a watery landscape Frankie could hardly see. A low grey sky pressed down on the wild Dorset heathland, giving it a desolate aspect, and in all the villages where the bus briefly stopped the streets were uninhabited, the houses firmly closed and silent. By the time it reached Canford Tarrant she was the sole remaining passenger.

'I'm looking for a place called Cerne Farm,' she told the driver before dismounting. 'All I know is that it's around here somewhere. Have you any idea exactly where it might be?'

'It be up that road there a little way,' he replied vaguely in a thick local accent. 'Just a short walk.'

Wheels splashing Frankie's boots and coat with mud, the bus trundled off, leaving her standing there, conscious of a sense of extreme isolation. The village consisted of a tiny Norman church and a huddle of stone and flint thatched-roof cottages beside a pond. There did not appear to be a shop or a pub where she could ask for more explicit directions, and there was no one about. She had no choice but to rely on the bus driver's knowledge.

The 'road' he had indicated was narrow and muddy, and although by now it was raining more heavily than ever, Frankie walked for a good twenty minutes, fairly sure that she had not missed any kind of dwelling. The sky was ominously dark on this grim late February day, and away in the distance she heard an unmistakable rumble of thunder. Worse still, a malicious wind had sprung up which rendered her umbrella virtually useless, driving the rain under it so that water trickled down unpleasantly beneath her collar.

The only indication that she was on the right track was a stile leading to a field, beside which a rough wooden sign pointed, bearing the legend 'Cerne Farm.' It must be somewhere near. But ten minutes further up the road Frankie still had not found it. Parting clouds gave her brief glimpses of the rising chalk downs, stretching away towards Cranbourne Chase, heath and moorland and occasional woody copse, lonely and unpeopled. She could not go on this way. Retracing her steps back to the stile, she decided to try the footpath across the fields. It was at least signposted to Cerne Farm, and might even be a short cut.

The path was even muddier than the road, not surprisingly. Frankie turned up her coat collar, lowered her umbrella until she could barely see in front of her, and trudged resolutely on.

'Damn this for a silly idea!' she muttered.

She had said as much—suitably paraphrased, of course—to Ivor Masterman when he had assigned her this task as if he were offering her a 'plum'. Which he probably imagined he was, for certainly he was expressing faith in her ability to handle different material.

'This is a completely new author to us, Frankie,' he had said, handing her the manuscript. 'Although his exploits are well known, it's the first time he has attempted to write them up in one volume. He has plenty to say, and a voice all his own.'

'Oh, but Ivor—exploration! *Boys' Own Paper* stuff! It's hardly my drop,' she had demurred. Why *me*, her unusual amber-brown eyes had pleaded their unspoken comment. My desk is as overflowing as anyone's, I have a full complement of writers under my aegis, and this is not my speciality. I need a new author who, in the way of new authors, will probably require kid-glove handling and lots of time-intensive encouragement like a hole in the head!

Ivor was a tiny, bespectacled gnome of a man, but he had a sawtooth of a mind, and what was more, he *was* Cooper Masterman, as his father had been before him. Blue ink flowed in his veins instead of blood, it was rumoured; his publisher's instinct was legendary and seldom mistaken. You could argue with him only so far, if you valued your job, which Frankie did. Keen and ambitious, she had fought her way to her editor's desk and was well aware that in this cut-throat world there would be a queue to fill it if she were foolish enough to put it in jeopardy.

So when he had said firmly, 'Frankie, I think you can do this, and it's time your perspectives were widened. Life isn't all actors' autobiographies and volumes of poets' letters,' she had shrugged her shoulders and capitulated, although not without a parting shot.

'OK—enough said. I'm on my way to deepest Dorset,' she had grimaced. 'But I still haven't grasped the logic of expecting someone like myself to establish rapport with a wild hero who goes dashing off disturbing remote places and peoples who would best be left alone. I'm a veteran of too many peace marches and protest movements.'

'That was when you were a student. It was a long time ago,' Ivor had observed pitilessly. 'Besides, I'm not one of those who believes that complete agreement between author and editor is always ideal. Sometimes, what is required is... an interaction. So go forth and interact.'

Ivor was not noted for his kindness! 'That was a long time ago' had reminded Frankie of her imminent thirtieth birthday, and lo and behold, that very morning she had peered in her bathroom mirror and tweezed out of her head what looked suspiciously like a grey hair! Surely not? A good job she was fair, and they wouldn't show too much when they did strike... perhaps a few subtle streaks would help...? Realising that if she didn't hurry she would be in danger of missing the train, she had quickly finished her make-up, but one way and another she was not in a good mood, and had viewed the day ahead with very little pleasure.

To be fair, Ivor had not given her a lot of time to read the manuscript, but her own reluctance had made her put it off until the last moment. It would have been very wrong, and against Frankie's firm scruples, to meet an author without having at least looked at his work, so she read it on the train. There were, as yet, only three chapters and a synopsis outlining the book's future development, and she read straight through, without the blue pencil in her hand. No good editor would make alterations or comments on a first reading, she felt, and she intended anyhow to go through it again with the writer.

Prejudiced as she was against the subject matter, she had had to hold out against a surprised, grudging interest. The author had led expeditions to many of the world's most dangerous and inhospitable places, and he wrote about them in a manner that was knowledgeable and unsentimental. Not only was his style clear and literate, but he possessed something more elusive, that rare ability to grip—what Frankie called the page-turning factor. A writer either had it or did not, and it was in her opinion unteachable. There were flashes, too, of a grim humour, sometimes almost black, that made her sit back in appreciative astonishment before reminding herself that she did not really care for this sort of thing.

Frankie did not follow newspaper write-ups of transpolar crossings or attempts to prove that the Pacific could be traversed by raft. To her, undertakings such as these were a waste of time and money which could be more valuably spent. Therefore she knew little of Julian Tarrant, and had no idea how he would look. But she had drawn a mental picture. He would be blustering, would probably sport a handlebar moustache, and would stalk about with a shotgun in one hand and two retrievers in tow. The trouble was, the picture was at variance with the voice which spoke to her so directly from the page, and she had to close her mind to one image in order to keep the other firmly fixed.

Now, trudging along the muddy path, wet, cold, windbattered and still not in sight of Cerne Farm, she had ceased, for the moment, to care about either the book or its author. All she wanted was to be warm, dry and somewhere else! To hell with Julian Tarrant! Anyone who chose to live somewhere as inaccessible and desolate as this had to be half crazed!

'Madam—I don't know where you think you're going, but you happen to be on my property.'

The mere sound of a human voice in these surroundings caused Frankie to pull up dead in alarm. She had begun to think Dorset was totally uninhabited, and to feel like an alien visitor on a dead planet. She'd had the umbrella held out in front of her, protecting her face from the onslaught of the wind and rain, and consequently, she had not even seen the man until he spoke. Raising it cautiously, she peered at him from beneath its dripping brim.

Frankie was tall, and it took a lot of man to make her feel fragile and threatened, but this individual was well-qualified. He towered over her by inches, and was powerfully made to boot, dressed in thick cord trousers and a green waxed three-quarter jacket, a floppy hat set at a rakish angle on his head, and under his arm he carried something unidentifiable, concealed by a tarpaulin cover. The cold, irritated displeasure in his voice carried over into a stern face, and although he didn't look as if he could be more than forty he spoke with the firm, no-nonsense manner of one being used to being obeyed.

For all he was the first human contact she'd had since getting off the bus, and she might well need him to direct her to her destination, Frankie's hackles rose, and she could not resist giving him back a little of his own disdainful unpleasantness.

'Oh, really? I hardly think one can be guilty of trespass following a public foot path,' she retorted with asperity.

He shifted the load under his arm only slightly, but the movement caused Frankie to take an involuntary step backwards, of which she was quite ashamed. She would not have him think she was frightened of him, whoever he was! From beneath the brow of his hat she caught an icy glitter of eyes the colour of which was indiscernible in this murk, but signalled an unwelcoming exasperation.

'You left the public footpath at the end of the first field—it branches off in the opposite direction,' he explained with strained patience. 'This stretch is private, and leads only to my house. I'll admit it's not easy to see one's way in such weather, but then, who goes for a country ramble in these conditions?'

This was tantamount to declaring that Frankie was off her trolley. It was quite bad enough to be cold, wet and lost, without having some strange, not very pleasant man accusing her of being crazy into the bargain.

'I am not out for a country ramble,' she retorted icily. 'Although I may well be on a fool's errand, tramping around searching for some character who's an amalgam of Dr Livingstone and Captain Scott, and who hasn't the nous to reside within hail of civilisation!'

It was his turn to pull up short, and he regarded Frankie, a frown compressing his brow and narrowing his eyes, so that it occurred to her fleetingly that he was not a man it would be advisable to cross, or to make an enemy of.

'This...er...character,' he said in a cold, cultured voice dripping derision. 'Where does he live? Precisely, I mean.'

Frankie stared back at him defiantly, but something inside her began to shrivel beneath the blast of his glowering scrutiny, and she was not a lady who was easily intimidated. Too many years in the rat race of publishing had equipped her to hold her own, so why was she in danger of quailing now?

'He lives at Cerne Farm, or so I was given to understand,' she said frostily, aware that in her anger she must have made the *faux-pas* of referring rudely to someone who was probably a neighbour of this man.

But his expression had changed to one of disgust.

'Oh, my God!' he said, raising scornful eyebrows, 'You're from Cooper Masterman? I'd given up on them, in view of the weather.'

Frankie wished that all five feet nine inches of her could slide down into her boots and disappear, for her *faux-pas* had been the even more classic one of insulting, unwittingly, the very same person she was supposed to meet, encourage, collaborate with and generally wet-nurse towards publication!

'Mr Tarrant?' she asked weakly.

'Julian Tarrant,' he confirmed. 'I was told to expect Frankie Somers, but if *he* couldn't make it, there was little point in his sending his secretary.'

This outrageously sexist assumption gave Frankie's flagging courage just the shot in the arm it needed. She drew herself up, unconsciously shaking the raindrops from the damp ends of her artfully layered short blonde crop.

'*I* am Frankie Somers,' she informed him haughtily. 'Frankie is short for Francesca, in case you needed to know that. It was *my* personal assistant who made the arrangements. I did try to make personal contact with you, but you were not available.' She risked a sarcastic little smile. 'It may be a man's world up the Limpopo,

Mr Tarrant, but in publishing circles it's unwise so to presume.'

Her pleasure in this little triumph was short-lived, for not only was he not amused, he was not even discomfited by his own error. In fact, he was highly indignant, as if a diabolical trick had been played on him, and she was responsible by virtue of being female.

'Good lord!' he said disgustedly. 'I thought I had chosen a reputable publisher! What the devil can they be thinking of, sending a woman editor? I'm writing about exploration, not a love story!'

In spite of the damp, biting cold, Frankie could feel a hot surge of humiliation and anger begin to wash over her. How was it possible, almost at the end of the twentieth century, for women still to be subjected to this kind of belittlement? In what dim recesses of the genetic tank were they still breeding the kind of man who thought this way?

'If that's the way you feel, Mr Tarrant, then you should have made it clear from the outset, and saved me a thoroughly wretched journey and both of us the waste of our time!' she flung acidly at him. 'As a matter of fact, I am fully capable of handling any kind of work. I certainly don't specialise in romance. I have read your manuscript, and I came here prepared to discuss it constructively. What I'm not prepared to do is to stand in the rain and be abused!'

This fine little speech was unfortunately ruined by a sudden fierce gust of wind which siezed Frankie's umbrella like the sails of a galleon and blew it inside out. Dropping her briefcase on the muddy grass, she wrestled with the recalcitrant spokes in a manner she knew made her look far from dignified, and worse, achieved no success.

Julian Tarrant set down his tarpaulin-covered burden, moving with amazing agility for so tall a man, and took the umbrella from Frankie with swift authority. He gave it a brisk shake, so that it righted itself instantly, and handed it back to her.

Somewhere during the transaction his fingers accidentally and unconcernedly brushed her wrist, between the top of her leather glove and her coat sleeve, and a weird sensation assailed her. He was so large and so close, and Frankie, who spent much of her life in dealings with men without being overawed or disturbed by them, was astounded and embarrassed to find that suddenly she was both. And he wasn't even likeable!

He picked up her muddied briefcase and handed her that, too, and taking it from him, she was careful to ensure that their hands did not touch.

'Thank you,' she said stiltedly, and with a lack of grace that would have made her ashamed of herself had not other emotions been so strong as to overpower such niceties.

'Not at all.' He appeared belatedly to have remembered his manners. 'Look—you're soaked. You had better come into the house, although I warn you, it isn't especially warm. The boiler packed up this morning and the repair man can't get here until tomorrow.'

She managed a tight smile and an attempt at sympathy.

'Repair men never can. You're lucky it's tomorrow and not Friday week,' she said.

He hoisted up his burden again.

'Luckily we have these,' he said. 'Logs for the open fire. We keep them in various caches here and there, but they are of no immediate use unless they are dry—hence the tarpaulin. Follow me. You'll have to excuse my back, but the path won't permit two abreast, and it makes sense if I lead the way.'

He set off at a brisk stride, and Frankie did the only sensible thing she could do in the circumstances. She followed. The path led over a gentle hill, and from the brow, looking down into the valley, she saw a large, rambling, grey-stone, thatch-roofed house standing quite alone. One sturdy estate car was parked outside on a drive bordered by rhododendrons which would be magnificent in summer. There were dripping lawns, dripping elms and beeches, but none the less she could see that this was a lovely spot, enfolded peacefully in the chalk downs.

Julian Tarrant opened the door she noted he had not troubled to lock, and stood aside briefly to allow her to precede him. Frankie shivered—he was right. It was an old house, and without any heating, clammily cold. There were oak beams everywhere and the ceilings barely cleared his height. Chintz curtains against the mullioned windows, matching loose covers and toning cushions on the upholstery, artfully hued lampshades and bowls of dried flowers in niches caught her eye. Ornaments and *objets d'art* tastefully displayed. A woman's touch everywhere, but no sign of any woman.

He knelt by the huge inglenook fireplace and began deftly constructing a pile of logs and paper in the grate, ignoring Frankie as if he had forgotten she was there, concentrating completely on his task. For some reason she failed to understand, this annoyed her, and as he touched a match to the paper and the flames leapt she said, a little dismissively, 'I always thought one rubbed two sticks together, or some such thing. How disappointing.'

'Perhaps, but I was never actually in the Scouts,' he said drily, and his failure to rise to the bait annoyed her even further.

Now that he had removed his hat, she saw that his hair was lighter than her own, almost a silver blond, and his eyes were ice-blue, distance-seeking, the kind of eyes from which you could hide very little. His was a face that spoke of experience and authority, and a deep, guarded, instinctive reserve. A face intriguingly lined, and quite out of the blue Frankie thought, This man has been to hell and back by several routes, but he would die before he would admit it. And he was younger than she had at first thought... no more than late thirties, she guessed.

Removing his coat, he indicated that she should do the same.

'I know it's cold, but sitting in wet clothes is bad for you,' he said. 'I'll hang them in the kitchen.'

In his absence Frankie went over to the window and looked out. It was only early afternoon, but the sky was as dark as pewter. The wind had sharpened to gale force and was driving the rain hard against the glass. She shuddered and returned gratefully to the infant fire, just as he came back, carrying an oil lamp that looked positively antique, but was glowing brightly.

'Don't you have any power on at all?' she asked, eyes widening.

'No. There were gales overnight and the electricity is knocked out. That's why the boiler isn't working,' he said. 'There's no gas here, so in effect everything is off. I had intended phoning your office to cancel the appointment, in view of the conditions, but then the phone went out of order as well. Do sit down, for heaven's sake. The fire will soon get going.'

Frankie subsided on to a comfortable settle in front of the hearth, and he crouched, balanced firmly on his heels, coaxing the logs into life. He wore a thick Aran sweater over the cords, and she found herself watching his wrist and forearm as he poked the fire. Powerful arms, with a faint down of blond hair, but, like the rest of him, she imagined faintly, spare and untroubled by flab. The perfect male machine.

What thoughts to be entertaining, for a woman who liked men but deemed it politic to trust them only as far as she could throw them! Frankie tore her attention away from the disturbing Mr Tarrant and made a point of watching the flames as they began to leap and crackle.

The house was far too quiet for any other life to be being lived within its walls. The silence had a permanence about it which led her to guess that the other occupants were not just out—they were non-existant. Her gaze strayed back to him, drawn there with hypnotic reluctance.

'Are you alone here, Mr Tarrant?'

'Yes,' he replied perfunctorily, and that was the end of it. No enlargement, no explanations. A man of few words, by habit? Or was he simply telling her to mind her own business? He was within his rights, she supposed, although the question was natural enough.

'Then if you have no gas in the house, and the electrics are off, how on earth are you going to be able to cook anything?' she asked, as the thought struck her.

'Your concern is touching, but unnecessary. I really don't need my mother with me,' he said testily. 'Man

managed to survive before he had all these modern re-
finements, you know, and I've had plenty of practice at
doing without them. Haven't you ever cooked over an
open fire?' His brows rose questioningly, and he
answered his own question, clearly labelling Frankie as
a couch potato. 'No, I don't suppose you have.'

Motherly was the last thing Julian Tarrant made
Frankie feel. She resented his male chauvinistic pigeon-
holing of her, beneath which she sensed a suspicion and
misunderstanding of her entire sex, and which she imagined must be the outcome of a man's life lived pre-
dominantly among men.

But that wasn't the whole of it, she felt. There was
something else she could not quite put her finger on,
but which bothered her—a brooding, angry dissatis-
faction, suppressed but not entirely hidden. And she
found his physical presence profoundly disconcerting,
which was odd, because he had in no way harassed her
sexually, or given any indication that he found her femi-
ninity anything but a nuisance.

Frankie had put far pushier men in their place with
an ease born of regularity—she could not have survived
as a single professional woman without acquiring this
technique. And Julian Tarrant was not a ladies' man.
He doesn't need to be, she surprised herself thinking
ruefully.

'You are speaking to one who has cooked *boeuf
bourguignonne* over a paraffin stove,' she informed him
loftily, and saw a truant flicker of something like
amusement enliven the chill cerulean depths of his eyes.

'Don't tell me you were a Guide leader?'

'No. Just a camper,' she corrected laconically. 'Holidays had to be inexpensive in the days when I was a student, and then a struggling junior editor.'

A brief curiosity showed itself on the stern, unemotional face, and she sensed him hesitating on the brink of asking her something about her personal life, the answer to which was in some way important to him. Then it subsided again just as swiftly, and the mask of indifference fell. He gave the logs on the fire a vicious poke and they collapsed into a glowing pile.

'Tea,' he said shortly. He disappeared into the kitchen and returned with a blackened and ancient aluminium kettle.

'A whole cupboard full of hi-tech gadgets in there, all of which are entirely useless in the present circumstances,' he said scathingly, and Frankie could not escape the feeling that it was more than the redundant technology he was lambasting. 'Fortunately, this old faithful, which is the veteran of many expeditions, will not desert me in my hour of need.'

He set it deftly atop the fire, fetched mugs, sugar, milk and teabags. The kettle whistled cheerfully in no time at all; the tea was hot, strong and very welcome. Frankie curled her cold hands around her mug and watched Julian Tarrant spoon sugar liberally into his.

'Ugh—you do realise what that stuff is doing to you, I presume?' she shuddered.

'God!' He gave a heavy sigh of impatient disgust. 'You're at it again! Why do women have this irresistible urge to tell men what's good for them?' he demanded.

Frankie assumed that the question was rhetorical, but she could not bring herself to let it pass unchallanged.

'You don't like women very much, do you?' she countered.

He shrugged.

'Women are fine—like airports, or six-lane motorways. It's the Not in My Back Yard syndrome,' he said. And actually grinned.

The smile ironed out the lines of his face and created a new one—a hollow just above his jawline which, when he was a small boy, might have been a dimple unexpectedly appeared. The effect was devastating, transforming the dour, stern, introverted individual into an attractive and appealing man any woman would pick out in a crowd and make a play for. Frankie, realising that she was staring at him, looked away, and then her eyes were drawn back again.

'Oh, dear! Then it's a good thing that I'm merely an editor—sex immaterial,' she said crisply.

Julian Tarrant looked at her—really looked, perhaps for the first time, with his mind not sidetracked by his malfunctioning heating system and whatever other problems and inconveniences were currently souring his disposition. His regard was direct and analytical, and she had the odd notion that if he were to turn away immediately he would have been able to describe her in minute detail, leaving out nothing. She had been reconnoitred.

'You must be joking,' he said with heavy scorn, but his eyes were steady and unflinching. It was many a year since a man had been able to make her squirm with embarrassment, and she fought the weakness now, staring back at him boldly, and refusing to admit, by an inch, that it made any difference to the job she was here to

do, or that the fact that he was large and powerful and
intensely masculine cowed her in the least.

He's trying to get rid of me, she thought suddenly,
full of angry humiliation. He had probably reasoned that
if he behaved in a hard, unfriendly, sarcastic manner
calculated to make her feel uncomfortable, she would
turn tail and run, and Cooper Masterman would then
replace her with someone else more to his liking. Which
obviously meant someone male!

Well, he had succeeded, in a sense—she *did* feel uncomfortable, but perhaps not in the way he might have
expected. His misogynist indifference, coupled with that
wry smile which creased his hard mouth into an unsuspected tenderness, his tough shell, calloused over the occasional treacherous fissure, his muscular yet elegant
body—all of this hit Frankie squarely in the solar plexus,
a region unstirred in her for so long she had considered
it defunct.

But he was not her kind of man at all. Far from it.
He belonged to a species she actively detested.

'Mr Tarrant,' she said as pleasantly as she could,
summoning up her best professional smile, reassuring
and businesslike, 'I assure you that I am quite serious.
Think of me solely as a working brain, and then it won't
matter that I am cluttering up your back yard for a short
while! Now, then—shall we get on? I have read through
the three extant chapters of your projected book, and if
we could go through it again together I could probably
make some suggestions and comments you might find
useful. Since I am here, we may as well take a look,
don't you think?'

'Oh, absolutely,' he said with dry, obviously feigned
earnestness. So now he had decided to poke fun at her,

had he, to make it clear he could not take her seriously? Frankie, outwardly ice-calm, was burning up with fury inside. She had never met a man whom she had found instantly so physically compelling, and who at the same time aroused in her an instinctive antagonism.

Fingers struggling to refrain from giveaway fumbling, she took the manuscript from her briefcase. Julian Tarrant pulled out a small coffee-table from a nest and set it in front of her, and with a brief, formal 'Thank you', she launched herself into her work without hesitation.

She went through the manuscript carefully, page by page, and he listened in silence as point by point she stated where small changes might lead to improvement, where she differed from him on a matter of style, and where she felt that perhaps some clarification was required. Still he said nothing, and after a while, his silence became unnerving.

'You will probably agree that they are all fairly minor niggles,' she observed, trying not to sound apologetic. After all, she was only doing her job as conscientiously as she could. 'For example, you deal with the expeditions you have led, and their historical backgrounds, which is fine. But I see from your synopsis that there is nothing about your most recent expedition— Amazonia, wasn't it? A short introduction dealing with that might be a suggestion. It would bring your account up to the present, and help readers relate to you more easily.'

A ripple of feeling creased the lines on his forehead more deeply.

'The book is not concerned with that expedition, or intended to be. In that sense, it's not current, but historical,' he said a little tersely, and her editor's instinct immediately picked up his reluctance. There were things he did not want to write about—perhaps not even to think about? The short hairs at the nape of Frankie's neck prickled with the sharply aroused interest of a terrier scenting a rabbit, and she was suddenly alert and concerned, for these were most likely the very factors which would bring his book roundly to life.

'History is the day before yesterday, Mr Tarrant,' she persisted.

Julian Tarrant uncurled his powerful frame and stood up with an abruptness which almost knocked the table over. His face as he looked down at Frankie was dark and tormented. Sorrow, guilt, anger—she could not untangle the emotions on it.

'That may be your opinion, but *I* am writing this book, and I'll include what I decide is pertinent, or I won't write it at all,' he said sharply. 'So if you don't mind, we'll leave it at that.'

Frankie had never before been spoken to in such a manner by a prospective author. Usually they were ready to take advice, and eager to be published above all. She was so surprised by his brusqueness and so shaken by the expression on his face that she shut up. But almost at once he appeared dry and disdainful, and when he spoke again his voice was level, if a little curt.

'I'm hungry right now, and that doesn't improve my temper,' he said. 'How about you?'

She watched in disbelief as this unpredictable man suspended literary discussion while he heated soup—from a can, she supposed, but it smelled good—in a saucepan over the fire, and produced a huge wedge of Stilton on a plate.

'Is there anything I can do?' she felt obliged to offer.

He looked her over measuringly, all to obviously deciding whether she might be capable of doing anything useful.

'Can you make toast?' he demanded.

Frankie's eyes lit up.

'In front of the fire? I haven't done that since I was a child!' she exclaimed delightedly. 'It's one of the pleasures central heating has robbed us of.'

Something about her ingenuous enthusiasm seemed to amuse him, and he smiled again, that briefly tender, melting smile. My God, thought Frankie, he didn't *have* to like women, he didn't even have to put himself out for them. He only had to smile that way. . .

'Here.' He handed her half a sliced loaf in a plastic bag and seized a toasting fork from a set of expensive copper fire-irons on the hearth.

Frankie was aghast.

'I can't use that, it's ornamental—for decorative purposes only!' she gasped.

'I've neither time nor use for anything that's purely decorative!' he declared fiercely. 'Get toasting, Ms Somers.'

'Yes, Mr Tarrant, sir!' she said with a touch of light mockery, glad that he could not observe the switchback current that rollercoastered down her spine from end to end.

A brief, injudicious student marriage had left Frankie divorced and disillusioned before her twenty-first birthday. Not that she blamed anyone but herself for this mistake. An unusually strong moral sense had made her resist Tom's insistence that she sleep with him, even though she thought she was in love. Attraction had proved too strong, and in a rash moment they got married. Not surprisingly, the basis was too flimsy for the relationship to last, and they had cut their losses and gone their separate ways.

Since then, pursuing an exacting career had demanded much of her time, energy and emotional resources, but it would have been unrealistic for her not to have had the occasional flirtation over the course of nearly a decade. She was normal. Human. She had no hang-ups other than a naturally cautious reluctance to be twice bitten. She could cope with anything in trousers, so she believed, and knew exactly how to judge the cutoff point beyond which loomed the dangers of too great an involvement. In short, she could take it, or she could leave it.

So why was she rocked back on her heels by the glacial-eyed, uncompromisingly brusque, rude, hostile, woman-hating Julian Tarrant, a man she could never like, who certainly did not like her, and who was as far as the distant stars from all that, in her opinion, a man should be?

CHAPTER TWO

THE thunderstorm which had been building up in the distance all afternoon broke suddenly and viciously over Canford Tarrant, rattling every window of Cerne Farm with its fierce reverberations. The sky was as black as pitch, a cloudburst of monsoon proportions poured relentlessly down, and a raging wind howled. Somewhere in the upper regions of the house, a door banged intermittently, an eerie, irritating noise which set Frankie's nerves on edge.

The soup and toast were finished, along with half the Stilton. Julian Tarrant opened a drop-fronted oak cupboard and got out glasses and a bottle of gin, splashing in generous measures and adding tonic. He did not trouble to ask Frankie first whether or not she wanted a drink, and, if so, what she would like.

'No ice, I'm afraid,' he said.

'Well, no, how could there be when the fridge isn't working?' Frankie commiserated.

'That's perceptive of you,' he observed drily.

The sarcasm was entirely unnecessary, and Frankie fought a wild moment of antagonism in which she seriously contemplated blowing this assignment, and probably her job as well, to kingdom come, by tossing the contents of her glass straight into his face. She had seen it done by heroines in old Hollywood movies, always to great dramatic effect, and it would have told Julian

Tarrant better than words ever could what she thought of him.

She resisted the temptation nobly, because her job was too important to imperil for a split-second of ecstatic satisfaction, and besides, it was certain he would not take kindly to such treatment. He was probably an expert in unarmed combat, and she might very likely find herself flat on her back on the carpet. Frankie's mind raced away with a vision of herself and the impossible man locked in a close grapple, his hard, powerful body pinning hers to the ground, his strong hands tight around her wrists, that mouth, with the muscle jumping beside it, an inch away from hers...

She took a large gulp of her drink, not caring that it burned her throat. She had not fantasised like this about a man she scarcely knew since she was a teenager!

''Strewth, Mr Tarrant, if you're this liberal with the gin, I bet you mix a mean martini!' she exclaimed. 'Now...er...to get back to your manuscript...'

It wasn't easy. The crashing tumult of the storm raging outside she could have ignored had she been sitting at her desk at Cooper Masterman. But she was alone in an empty house lit only by firelight and flashes of eerie lightning, and the glow of an oil lamp. Isolated, miles from anywhere and anyone, alone with a man who was virtually a stranger, who made her nerves rasp and twitch. Anything could happen...

Stop it, Frankie! she told herself sternly. How many men had she been alone with in the course of her work, without suffering this kind of childish reaction? *Nothing* would happen, because Julian Tarrant was not looking for any such encounter—quite the reverse. So why did she feel so endangered?

He reached across the table to turn a page, pointing back to a paragraph which illustrated a point he had just made. Frankie's eyes followed the progress of his hand with covert fascination. It was a large, capable hand, long-fingered, nails blunt-cut and fastidiously clean.

She figured him for a perfectionist, meticulous as to detail, demanding in the extreme with regard to both his relationships and his environment. Whoever cleaned his house for him, it was immaculately done; nothing was out of place. She did not think living alone would faze him, or that there was anything he could not manage for himself, but she wondered again about his personal life. This was no bachelor pad... so had he ever been married? She did not think it politic to ask.

He caught her eye, almost as if he suspected she was puzzling about matters outside her brief, but there was nothing defensive about his stare. Go ahead and ask, it challenged her, just try it... Frankie declined, but she did not look away, and as the silence lengthened between them in contrast to the din of the storm raging outside, and the unspoken confrontation persisted, something very odd happened.

This man who did not care for women... no, who seemed to nurse a positive resentment against them... suddenly had a gleam in his chilly blue eyes that was quite different from the cold, combative gaze of a second ago.

Shock-waves ran up and down Frankie's spine, and an acute awareness of herself left her vulnerable as never before. Almost, she saw herself through his eyes... the fashionably shaggy short crop of wheat-coloured hair atop a face that was interesting and vivacious rather than conventionally pretty, the large amber eyes its most striking feature...the tall, slim body, essentially female, endless legs outlined by the tailored skirt of her navy suit, jacket open, revealing an ivory silk shirt flatteringly draping the generous line of her breasts.

She saw Julian Tarrant taking in all of this with clinical male appreciation, and in that instant knew that it was entirely possible that he might suddenly close the slight distance between them and take her in his arms. Crazy as it seemed, it might happen, and the realisation hovered dangerously in the air around them.

What worried her far more profoundly was the possibility that she might not be of a mind to stop him if he did. That she might actually welcome and enjoy it...

She stacked the pages of the manuscript together with a swift movement deliberately engineered to snap the build-up of tension in the atmosphere between them.

'I think that's perhaps as far as we should attempt to go today,' she said briskly. There was no double meaning intended in her words, but his mouth twitched very slightly in an infuriating parody of a smile.

'Absolutely,' he said again, as he had before, and in the same drily mocking tone, and Frankie did not know if she were more furious with him or with herself. He looked calculatedly at his watch. 'In fact, Ms Somers, if you want to get home tonight, I suggest you make a move.'

Make a move? Frankie's expressive mouth fell open and she shot a swift glance out the window. Driving rain all but obscured the world beyond, but the wind still howled, and somewhere not too far away a rumble of thunder declared that the storm's fury was not yet spent.

'Certainly I want to get home,' she said, 'but have you seen it out there? Do you suggest I wear flippers and a snorkel?'

He said patiently, 'I was merely making the point that the last bus leaves Canford Tarrant at five, and after that, without one's own transport, there's no way out. Since you can't stop here, there doesn't seem to be any alternative to catching it.'

Frankie glared at him, waves of antagonism all but overwhelming her.

'I have no desire whatsoever to be marooned here overnight,' she said icily. 'The prospect does not appeal, believe me! But I find it hard to accept that you don't have a spare room in this great mausoleum of yours, or that you couldn't put someone up in an emergency. Just for the record, I should not be in the least afraid of compromising my virtue or my reputation!'

Julian Tarrant suffered this outburst with patient indifference.

'You may not be, but I am,' he said bluntly. At Frankie's outraged gasp, he sighed resignedly. 'All right—for the record—I'm contesting my ex-wife for greater access to my children. I can't afford the indiscretion of having a woman under my roof all night. One could say no one would know, but this is the country. Someone always knows.'

Frankie's anger deflated like a pricked balloon as she accepted, not without reluctance, the effort this explanation had cost him. She realised afresh that this man had known pain and was not as self-contained as his hard-coated exterior led one to believe.

'I didn't mean to invade your privacy,' she said quietly, 'nor do you have to push me out of the door. I had every intention of going, regardless of the weather. I was just . . . annoyed.'

'Get annoyed easily, do you?' he hinted, the crease at the side of his mouth deepening.

'Not at all,' Frankie contradicted huffily. 'On the whole I would say I'm an even-tempered, fairly tolerant individual.'

'Mmm,' he said, and now there was most definitely humour lurking in his voice. 'I know what you mean. I'm generally a peaceable fellow myself.'

Frankie objected to the underlying mockery of his words. She objected to the feeling that he was sending her up, and that every time she attempted to fight back he struck out and demolished her.

'I find that hard to swallow!' she said scathingly. 'Peaceable fellows don't go blundering about in remote corners of the globe, disturbing the inhabitants who would much rather be left to themselves.'

He regarded her measuringly, quite unruffled.

'There is little harm done by people like myself, who treat wild places with respect and by and large leave them as we found them,' he said coolly. 'Cosy intellectuals like you, who turn their backs and pontificate whatever rubbish they choose out of the depths of their ignorance are far more dangerous.'

He turned away from her abruptly.

'You're right. You can't walk through this. I'll drive you to the bus.'

It was a relief to Frankie to be back in the warmth and security of her narrow Victorian house not far from Clapham Common. She kicked off her boots in the hall, which was cluttered with piles of books and sundry footgear that had not found its way home yet, and in her stockinged feet ran upstairs to her bedroom, where she hung her wet coat in the airing cupboard and her suit jacket in the wardrobe before going back downstairs. In the living-room the central heating had already come on, as it was programmed to do. Frankie drew the curtains and popped her ready-prepared casserole into the microwave. Before too long, she was settling gratefully into her favourite armchair, her dinner on a tray on her lap, feet stretched out, letting the warmth seep back into her body.

Warm, comfortable and well-fed, she spared a guilty thought for Julian Tarrant, alone in his unheated house, throwing logs on the fire to combat the icy chill, and heating up cans of soup.

He had driven her to the village in a terse silence which she had not seen fit to break, arriving just in time for her to catch the bus.

'I'll be in touch—about the manuscript,' Frankie had just found time to say quickly.

He had merely shrugged, as if to indicate that it was of no great importance to him whether she did or did not, whether he finished the book or shoved it in a drawer and forgot about it, or indeed, if it ever saw the light of day.

In which case, why write it? Frankie had puzzled as the bus laboured through the rain-soaked Dorset countryside. He had seemed committed to the project as they discussed it, and it would be a pity if he did abandon it at this stage. He wrote well and had interesting things to say. And yet . . . there was a detachment about him which Frankie could not breach.

She needed to know more about him if she was to work with him successfully. She needed to understand what made him tick, what motivated him to write at all. Most authors, in her experience, were only too happy to talk about themselves. But Julian Tarrant had divulged only one morsel of personal information, and that he had flung at her with angry reluctance.

Thus she knew he had been married and was now divorced—presumably quite recently, since he was still pursuing matters such as access rights. As he was still in residence at Cerne Farm, that beautiful house which showed all the hallmarks of a woman's exquisite taste, she guessed that Mrs Tarrant had left him, taking their children with her.

Snuggling down under her duvet that night, Frankie thought rebelliously, good for her! Who could live with a man like that.

But wait—suppose . . . just suppose . . . that it was her defection which had brought about that aloof, hostile demeanour, that deep resentment of all women? On the brink of sleep, Frankie was instantly wide awake again, transfixed by the notion that Julian Tarrant might be suffering from that commonplace but all too painful ailment, a broken heart.

She did not care for the fact that suspecting he did not hate all women *per se*, but loved one too much, prevented her from settling down to the peaceful sleep she so much needed after such an exhausting day. But she was honest enough to admit, in the still reaches of the night, that this was so.

He's not for you, she told herself firmly. Any such involvement would be a sure recipe for disaster, no doubt. Nevertheless, for some time her mind played and replayed those few moments when their eyes had held, and physical contact had seemed no more than a heartbeat away.

Just because we were alone, I was female, and I was *there*, she thought disgustedly. There was no way she would let any man make love to her on those terms—was there? Turning over and savagely pumelling her pillow into a more comfortable position, Frankie resolutely closed her eyes.

The rain which had engulfed the whole of southern England the previous day had cleared by morning, but the sky was still grey and sullen as Frankie arrived at Cooper Masterman's offices not far from Baker Street.

After a restless night she felt far from refreshed, but it made no difference to the punishing schedule ahead of her. Ivor Masterman expected his staff to be on their toes at all times, and Frankie had a nine-thirty appointment with him, which gave her only enough time to grab a quick cup of coffee and flip through her mail as Sally, her personal assistant, opened it.

'Any alarms in my absence?'

'Not really.' Sally slit another envelope and unfolded the letter on top of the pile on the desk. A steady, reliable young woman, she was Frankie's prop and stay, more of a friend than a subordinate. 'Himself was in a foul mood all day, so watch out when you go into the lion's den. What sort of a day did you have?'

Frankie groaned.

'Don't ask! It was simply awful,' she said ruefully. 'The journey was ghastly—it never stopped raining. The house was in the middle of nowhere, and freezing cold. As for the new author, Julian Tarrant, a more self-opinionated, arrogant, unpleasant man I have yet to meet!'

Sally's eyes danced curiously and her brown curls joined in.

'Wow! Was he handsome?' she demanded interestedly. Her efforts to give Frankie's romantic life a nudge had increased as the years passed, and she clearly saw the options decreasing.

Frankie gave a wry grin.

'I have to admit, he was, in a way,' she said. 'But handsome is as handsome does, and Mr Tarrant does not! Ugh—I'm more than half inclined to tell Ivor Masterman this is one I can't handle.'

'But you won't give in so easily, I know you won't,' Sally said seriously. 'You know it, too, so why say it?'

There was no sense in arguing with Sally, who knew her too well, and had shared many of her ups and downs, her triumphs and disasters with fierce partisanship, so Frankie merely grinned. There were other editors at Cooper Masterman who would clamour to look after Julian Tarrant if she turned him down, and she told herself she would like to see them try! He was capable of having any one of them for breakfast and spitting out the pips.

'Incidentally, you must have been a bit ambiguous about my sex when you made the arrangements,' she pointed out. 'It might be necessary to be more explicit in future. It seemed that our friend Mr Tarrant was expecting a man, and he was slightly miffed when I turned up.'

Sally was clearly astounded.

'I'm sorry—it never occurred to me that it mattered,' she gasped.

'Nor to me, but there are still some people to whom it obviously does,' Frankie said grimly, and then it occurred to her that Julian Tarrant might decide this issue for himself. He might very well ring up—once his phone line was restored—and tell Ivor that no, he specifically could not work with a female editor.

She was astonished by the sharp stab of apprehension this possibility caused her, the awareness that she would be quite severely disappointed if it were to happen. *She did not like this man.* He antagonised and infuriated her. They had nothing in common, quite the contrary, and she knew in her bones that he was going to be difficult to work with. She should get down on her knees and pray for deliverance.

Instead, she sailed into Ivor's *sanctum sanctorum* wearing a brisk professional attitude and exhibiting a confidence in herself she was far from feeling.

'Sit down, Frankie, don't tower over me,' Ivor commanded. He was five feet four, and even when seated conscious of his lack of stature, for which he compensated with a Napoleonic wielding of power.

Frankie sat and waited, trying not to bite her lip, while he concentrated frowningly on a report on his desk. Finally he looked up and across the desk at her, his eyes giving away nothing behind his thick spectacles, and said without preamble, 'Mr Tarrant phoned half an hour ago.'

'Oh,' Frankie said, aiming for a note which suggested interest without undue concern. 'He was incommunicado yesterday.'

'So he told me. He apologised for the appalling conditions you were obliged to put up with, and says you coped gallantly.'

Not even Julian Tarrant, Frankie thought un-
graciously, could hold himself responsible for the
weather, and here he was, apologising for it as if he personally had arranged for the storm, to test her endurance! Furthermore, she did not feel she had coped
'gallantly' at all. She was convinced this was just a sop,
thrown her way to sweeten the forthcoming rejection of
her services.

'Tell me the bottom line, please, Ivor,' she sighed. 'Mr
Tarrant has requested that you send him another editor—
preferably one who wears trousers, has a moustache, and
smokes a pipe.'

Ivor's sharp little eyes glittered fractionally, pinning
Frankie to her seat.

'I wonder what makes you say that?' he mused glee-
fully. 'No, as a matter of fact he seems to have been
quite impressed, and is keen to press on with his book—
with you as his guide and mentor.'

It was not good policy to allow Ivor to catch one out
in an error of judgement or miscalculation, and Frankie
knew that sooner or later she would be kicking herself
for her unguarded outburst. Right then, she could only
sit, silent and dumbfounded, while a multiplicity of
emotions washed over her. Triumph—despite the fact
that they had not hit it off personally, Julian Tarrant
must have had sufficient faith in her abilities to wish to
proceed, and he was not, she reasoned, a man to be easily
fooled or convinced of anything. Amazement, for she
had never expected anything remotely resembling praise
from this prickly, arrogant, difficult man.

Yes? Anything else?

Relief. Sheer, undeniable, overwhelming relief, because had he said that he was very sorry but he could

not work with her, she most likely would never have seen him again. It was this last response which troubled her.

She had made no reply to his last remark, and Ivor said sharply, 'Is this likely to present you with any problems, Frankie?'

'No,' she said quickly, conscious that this was the last point at which she could reasonably withdraw without upsetting the whole delicate apple-cart of author/publisher relations. Ivor would have been annoyed, of course, and in that mental notebook where he recorded marks for and against his employees she would have dropped several places down the scale. He would most certainly have held it against her, and it would not have been a brilliant career move.

But she could have done it. She could have said, 'Look, I could handle the material, but there is a personality conflict which might make it difficult for me to work with this particular author.' Such a thing did occasionally happen, although it had never before happened to Frankie, who prided herself on her ability to get along with most people.

So now she had committed herself to Julian Tarrant and his work, and that meant she also had to take on board his moods, his temper, his cold antipathy...and that discomfiting extra factor she had not bargained for...her own irrational and totally unexpected physical attraction to him.

'Sally,' she said to her PA, the minute she got back to her office, 'I want you to spend some time finding out all you can for me about Julian Tarrant. His background, his career, and such personal information as is available. Drop everything else for now and make this a priority.'

Sally's eyes widened.

'Sure, if you say so. But there are all these letters you said had to be answered as soon as possible.'

'They can wait. I'll take the dictaphone home with me and answer them tonight; you can type them up tomorrow,' Frankie said decisively. Forewarned was forearmed, and she had to know more about this man.

It made interesting reading. Julian Tarrant was Dorset born and bred, his family having farmed the land around the village that partly shared their name for several generations. Landed squirearchy, Frankie guessed. He had attended a minor public school, then Oxford, followed by a short commission in a commando regiment.

And then, against all expectations that might have been raised by such a background, he had seemingly refused to settle to a pattern. The world's wildest, most unexplored and dangerous regions had drawn him irresistibly—the polar ice-caps, deserts, unmapped mountain ranges. The scientific data he had gleaned from his expeditions were snapped up gratefully by the international bodies who increasingly often sponsored him, but it was the hazards he endured which drew coverage in magazines and newspapers. His last foray, just the previous year, had taken him deep into the still mysterious forests of Amazonia, and on this Sally had been able to find Frankie precious little information, beyond a brief, terse statement to the Press that owing to health problems he had decided to retire from this kind of activity.

As regards his personal life, all she learned was that he was married with a son and a daughter, and that detail had not been updated to include his recent divorce. An intensely private man.

Frankie tapped her pen on the desk, frowning. It was
the merest skeleton, and did not tell her why he was now
sitting in an empty house in Dorset, writing up the story
of every expedition he had ever led, apart from the last
one. The very omission of it was enough to grip her
interest. And what were the health problems which had
made him decide that there would be no more such ad-
ventures? He had looked strong, robust and fit as a fiddle
to her. What impulse had motivated him to put pen to
paper? Sentiment? Regret? Therapy for a failed marriage? There were a number of possible answers, and
they were all guesswork, but she doubted that he would
divulge any more. She would have to proceed inch by
inch in the dark, treading very carefully.

Sally came in, and caught her still frowning absently
into space.

'Oh dear,' she said. 'I don't think all that info I found
you has made you feel much happier, has it?'

'Not a lot,' Frankie confessed, and Sally smiled
sympathetically.

'Let's face it, this is hardly your thing. Intellectuals
are more your scene than men of action,' she observed.
'You look like one very harassed lady.'

Frankie shook herself. Was that how she appeared—
harassed and worried? If so, she would have to snap out
of it. It was all right for Sally to be aware of her doubts
and fears, but they must not go any further. Cooper
Masterman was no different from any other workplace
in that there were always people ready to capitalise on
the troubles of others.

It's just another book, she told herself forcefully. And
Julian Tarrant was just another author. She was an experienced and highly professional editor. She would give

him as much help and encouragement as she could, because if she was to be of any use to him at all her efforts had to be unstinting, with nothing held back.

As for her personal feelings ... animosity, misunderstanding, clashes of temperament ... these had to be endured ... indeed, they had to be set aside. She could do it, she insisted. And if she brought this project to successful fruition, how much more of a triumph it would be, how much more personal satisfaction she would be able to derive from it, knowing she had worked through and in spite of these difficulties, and succeeded none the less.

Gazing blankly at the opposite wall of her office, she seemed to see before her Julian Tarrant's icy patrician profile, its classic hauteur flawed intriguingly by that hollow above his jawline, his alert, vigilant blue eyes fixed on her.

'Oh, absolutely,' she seemed to hear him say in answer to her pious mental ramblings, instantly debunking them.

Even in his absence, her profound and violent response to his coldly abrasive humour, the intense physical charisma he wielded without knowing or caring about the extent of its power, came back to haunt her. She relived again that convulsive moment when she had truly not known whether she wanted to slap his face, be seized unceremoniously in his arms, or both.

Could she cope with these frightening and quite unwanted reactions? The only way was to be glacially calm and unemotional, to make it evident to him and to herself that he did not arouse her to anger or desire.

Get a grip on yourself, Frankie, she muttered to herself. You are a mature woman, you know the score, and you should be well past the stage of adolescent lusting. He's only a man!

Which was, she thought wryly, akin to saying the adagio from Beethoven's third symphony was only a tune. True, but far, far from the whole story.

CHAPTER THREE

FRANKIE'S life was far too busy and hectic to allow her unlimited time to spend brooding about Julian Tarrant or matters connected with him. Since she preferred not to think about him, this was all to the good. But she would have been lying had she said that he did not invade her thoughts at all. He did, and usually at unbidden and entirely inconvenient moments.

However, several weeks passed before she actually heard anything from him, and even then, annoyingly, the contact was not direct.

March had been a bitterly cold, rainy month, the kind of weather that lifted no one's spirits and made people who lived and worked in the capital tight-lipped and grumpy as they struggled to go about their business, waiting blue-faced on draughty tube platforms and dashing out of overheated shops into the icy blast of a fierce north wind.

Frankie had been out to lunch with an author, and over the Parma ham and melon and the supreme of chicken had spent most of the time trying to explain gently why, in her opinion, the lady's latest offering was not working, and required not merely a re-vamp but a total rewrite. It had been hard going, requiring much patience and diplomacy, and as she made her way back to the office along the cold, wet streets she felt that she had been through the mill.

'What I need is a cup of tea, the sooner the better!' she gasped, collapsing at her desk. Never mind that she had had two cups of overpriced espresso after lunch—the only thing that would satisfy her now was a hot, strong, reviving brew of tea, and Sally, who had doubtless anticipated this demand, already had the electric kettle on.

'Mr Tarrant phoned while you were out,' she said, placing the mug carefully on Frankie's desk, as if to soften the blow.

Frankie's nerves went on instant red alert. She gulped the hot liquid, swallowing hard to settle them, and burned her throat instead.

'Hell's bells! What does *he* want?' she spluttered, reaching for the Kleenex box.

Sally waited diplomatically until Frankie's coughs had subsided before saying, 'In a word—you. He needs to confer with you over chapter four, which he has finished, and chapter five, on which he's about to embark but which is causing him one or two problems. He says that it's not convenient for him to discuss it over the phone, and he has to see you personally.'

'Oh, dear,' Frankie groaned laconically. 'It looks like another trip to Dorset in the rain. Let's hope he's had the heating fixed!'

Sally shook her head.

'You're a bit luckier this time,' she grinned. 'He isn't in Dorset at the moment. He's staying somewhere in southern France. He didn't leave a number, but he said he would phone back soon.'

Frankie stared.

'He's where? Does he expect me to go chasing all over Europe after him?' she grumbled.

'Why not? You went all the way to California last year to see Lorna Greenbaum,' Sally pointed out reasonably. 'France is only a hop and a skip away. Most people would be only too delighted for a chance to get away from all this for a while.' She indicated the dismal scene outside the window. 'No chance of your requiring an assistant along, I suppose? No, I guess not!'

When Julian finally came on the line, Frankie waited until Sally was back in the big outer office where all the editorial secretaries and assistants worked, then she carefully closed the door before picking up the receiver. Why she troubled to take all these precautions, she wasn't too sure. Although she knew Sally didn't listen in to her calls, anyone walking past might be able to, she supposed. But what did she have to say to Julian Tarrant that the world couldn't hear?

In the intervening time before the switchboard put the announced call through to her, Frankie sat gripping the receiver and trying not to wonder what Julian was doing in France. Whenever she had thought of him, she had imagined him at Cerne Farm, and she was annoyed by her own naïve surprise on realising that he, too, had a life involving other places and other people. He could not spend the entire time he wasn't incarcerated at the farm working on his book tramping round the wet countryside being rude to people who inadvertently stepped over his boundaries.

'Hello.' His voice was as well remembered as if she had just left him, deep, strong and every bit as brusque.

'Mr Tarrant.' Frankie took a deep breath. 'I'm sorry I was out when you phoned, but it was my lunch hour. I gather you want to consult me about the next two chapters of your book?'

'That's correct. There are things we should go over before I proceed further, and, as I told your assistant, I'm afraid it can't be dealt with over the telephone,' he said, and the way he put it, it sounded to Frankie as if he would have been happier if the entire undertaking could have been accomplished without his having to see her at all!

'I see,' she said coolly, asking herself why, if that were true, she should trouble to cross the street in order to help him. 'Isn't there any likelihood of your being back in England in the near future? I am rather busy.'

'Not a chance,' he replied curtly. 'Unless the friends who are renting me the house decide to throw me out. The weather at home is unmitigatingly foul, so I'm told, and I'm quite comfortable where I am. What's the problem? Editors are usually prepared to visit authors wherever they happen to be, are they not?'

Frankie did not care for his authoritatively demanding tone. This was clearly a man used to giving orders and having them obeyed unquestioningly, but she wasn't a porter on one of his expeditions, and she objected to being summoned in this manner. The fact that he was making a perfectly reasonable request incensed her all the more.

'They are,' she admitted tautly, 'but I shall have to get my PA to look in my diary and see how I'm fixed. I can do that now, if you would care to wait.'

'I wouldn't care to. It's all the same to me when you come,' he said offhandedly. 'I shall be here, anyhow, so just drop me a line and let me know when you will be arriving. But make it soon, and plan on spending a few days. Meanwhile I'll post you directions on how to find me. The place where I am staying is rather off the beaten track.'

'I wouldn't expect visiting you ever to be simple,' she said drily.

'Not for you, Ms Somers, certainly,' he agreed, and rang off.

Frankie glared at the phone as if it were personally responsible for the irritation she was feeling, then she slapped it down angrily. That man! The rudeness, the arrogance, the downright effrontery of him! Just who did he think he was?

He thought he was an author, with a right to his editor's professional services, she answered her own question soberly. *She* was the one with the problem, here. He was not asking her to do anything she had not done a hundred times, even if his manner of asking was not to her liking.

'A trip to the nice, warm south of France to talk to a good-looking man, and you don't want to go?' Sally said half teasingly when Frankie asked her to check the diary. She shook her head at such lunacy. 'Come on— don't you fancy him just a little?'

'Me—fancy *him*? What a question!' Frankie retorted hotly.

'Yes, and one which you haven't really answered,' Sally said with a knowing grin.

Frankie stood up abruptly.

'I'm surprised at you, Sally, for even considering such nonsense!' she exclaimed. 'I am merely going to see an author, who happens to be male—fifty per cent of my authors are, in common with the rest of the population! If you had ever met Julian Tarrant, you would understand why any woman with an ounce of sense would give him a wide berth!'

After delivering this tirade, she turned her back and stalked stiffly out of the office, leaving a heavy, puzzled silence behind her.

In the corridor she sighed, leaned against the wall, and ran agitated fingers through her already tousled locks. This was becoming slightly ridiculous, she thought guiltily. Had the subject of discussion been anyone other than Julian Tarrant, she would have laughed and made a joke of Sally's comments. Instead, she had completely lost her self-control and sounded off at her assistant quite unnecessarily.

She would apologise to Sally for her sharpness once she had calmed down—of course she would. But that was not the point. What troubled her was that the first casualty of her professional relationship with Julian Tarrant had been her sense of humour. Or perhaps, more seriously, her honesty.

But what should she have said? Yes, in a way, I *do* fancy him, and at the same time I can't abide him ... he disturbs me and arouses in me feelings I don't know how to fight? She wasn't ready to confide such feelings to anyone. She wasn't even sure she understood them herself, in the full maturity of her own womanhood.

Nevertheless, three days later she had a flight booked to Toulouse, a hire car waiting for her there, and a precisely worded page of directions written by Julian Tarrant himself stuffed in her handbag. And she was on her way.

Most authors—most *people*—Frankie corrected herself as she cruised along the Autoroute de Deux Mers, gradually getting used to driving on the right, would have offered to meet her at the airport.

Julian Tarrant, for all he required her services, obviously did not think she merited such courtesy, and he had left her to make her own way. Still, that was just what she would have expected from him, and there was always a grim satisfaction in having one's worst opinions confirmed.

She tore her thoughts away from her ongoing annoyance with Julian and concentrated instead on the country unfolding around her. She knew Paris, Burgundy and the Loire valley, but not this more southerly part of France, and it was easy to discern, as soon as she smelled the faintly herb-scented air and felt the surprising warmth of the spring sun, that here she was in another world.

Beyond Toulouse, the Midi began—the ancient lands of the Languedoc which had once, in the Middle Ages, been a separate kingdom where a different tongue was spoken. As she drove south, the level land and the lower slopes of the hills either side of the road were thickly cultivated with young vines, but the higher reaches were drier and more sparse, the colour of gold or pale honey as the sun shimmered on them. Garrigue country, with a hint of wildness about it, scattered with perched, fortified villages where the populace had once taken refuge from marauding bandits and feuding armies.

At a motorway stopping point she bought a sandwich which was more like half a baguette, filled with ripe tomatoes, thick *jambon* and creamy mayonnaise, and a small bottle of mineral water. There were wooden tables under the trees, but Frankie did not feel like eating among the animated French families who were picnicking all around, so she pressed on. She was rewarded a few kilometres further on by the ideal spot, an *aire de repos* from where, pulling off the road, she could gaze at a not too distant view of the perfectly restored mediaeval city of Carcassonne.

Atop its lofty hill, and clearly visible for miles around, the massive walls encircling the old city, with their towers and battlements all looking much as they must have looked hundreds of years ago, it made her catch her breath in awe. A hard, weathered country with a violent past—a suitable background for Julian Tarrant, she could not help thinking.

Finishing her alfresco lunch, Frankie turned with some distaste to the directions he had sent her. According to him, she could have flown either to Toulouse or to Montpellier, but either way she would have had a fair drive on arrival. Now, as she left the motorway and set off into the wilder hinterland, she knew what he had meant.

At first, vineyards and olive groves and fields of fruit trees in early blossom flanked her route, and she passed through drowsy hamlets where very little stirred in the post-noon hush, save for the occasional sleeping dog disturbed by her car's engine, or here and there a black-clad granny watching her from the shade of a doorway.

But after a while she left behind her even such civilisations as this. Julian's route struck off from one such village up a lonely road between high, bleached hills. A ruined Saracen castle perched at a dizzy height frowned down at her as if her presence shattered the long sleep of its history. Frankie frowned back, shifting the unfamiliar gears of the hire car, which had an irritating tendency to stick as she ground down to second for the ascent. She hoped fervently that it did not have any more serious problems. A breakdown here would be a calamity.

She studied the neatly drawn map, searching for the right turn he had indicated. A road even narrower, even bumpier, led off into a desolate distance. Surely this could not be it?

I am heartily sick of playing hide and seek with this man, she thought exasperatedly, but she could not escape the conviction that if Julian Tarrant had said you turned right here, then right you turned. He was too precise and thorough to be vague about such things, and a man who had negotiated polar wastes would not have made a mistake on a simple continental route.

Several suspension-jerking miles further on, however, she was beginning to have her doubts, and kept driving only because there seemed to be no reasonable alternative. The road began to descend again, and with rising hope she saw olive groves and orchards once more. Signs of cultivation must mean that someone lived near by, and at the very least she might find someone to ask if she was going the right way.

Another hundred yards and her heart gave a surprised lurch. Beyond the trees stood a house—a bare golden shell of the same tawny stone as the Saracen castle and the houses in the villages she had passed along the way. Somewhere, a goat bleated and crickets hummed in the stubby grass, but she could discern no human life anywhere.

Frankie pulled up in front of the house and consulted Julian's map again. According to the spot he had marked on it, she had reached her destination, and certainly this was the only dwelling she had seen for some considerable time. It was isolated and not very elegant, but then, she had hardly expected Julian to be staying in a *village de vacances* with a heated pool and discos three times a week!

Getting out of the car, she approached the house cautiously. Her arrival was unnoticed, unheralded, but as she reached the front door, sure enough, she saw that there was a note pinned to it.

Ms Somers. Make yourself at home. Your room is at top of stairs on left, shower room down the corridor. Back later. J. Tarrant.

Of all the bare-faced nerve, thought Frankie, staring at the note with such outrage in her eyes it was a wonder it did not burst spontaneously into flames. She had come all this way at his request, and he could not even bother to be here when she arrived!

Picking up her bag, Frankie pushed the door and it opened at once. Julian Tarrant, she recalled, never seemed to lock doors. Perhaps he believed that no one would have the effrontery to rob a house where he was living! It felt strange to be walking into a place where she was expected, but which was empty. She made her way quietly along a stone-flagged hall, catching glimpses of an old-fashioned kitchen and a spacious but only partly furnished lounge along the way. It was rustic in the extreme, all the floors had the original tiles, cracked in places, and the furniture looked as if it had been picked up at local junk shops, but Frankie had to admit that it had a certain endearing charm about it, all the same.

Her bedroom, when she found it, had a narrow single bed, a wardrobe, and a chair and desk. She heaved her bag on to the bed, and decided that she really must shower off the grime of travel and change into clean clothes—and she had best be quick about it! The very last thing she needed was to be halfway through the process when Julian Tarrant arrived back from wherever he had gone. Locating the *salle d'eau*, she showered briskly, washed her hair and replaced the trousers and tunic she had travelled in with a straight sheath dress, cream with coffee-coloured trim and buttons down the front. It was new. In fact, she had treated herself to a quick shopping spree before coming out here, and had several new outfits.

'To impress this man whom you don't like,' Sally had said, inspecting the contents of her carrier bags.

'That has nothing to do with it. Spring is coming, and it's time I had some new clothes,' Frankie had retorted defiantly.

The cream sheath was her favourite. It skimmed her hips, emphasised the outrageous length of her shapely legs, and made her feel every inch a woman, elegant and professional at the same time. But now, surveying herself in the faded, speckled mirror on the back of her wardrobe, she was no longer sure of it, herself, or the effect she had desired to create.

She felt uncomfortably at odds with her surroundings, dressed up as for a smart city drinks party, out here in the wilds, in this lonely house where her host was not even present. It would have been no more than common courtesy for him to have been here to greet her when she arrived. That would not have been asking too much. Instead, he had chosen to absent himself. Didn't he care at all that she was the representative of the company who were to publish his book, or was he as indifferent to her offical capacity as he was to her personally?

Frankie winced. Perhaps she simply had to accept that Julian Tarrant did not like her, and had only tolerated her invasion of his sleepy southern hide-out when it could no longer be deferred. Well, it was mutual, she insisted. She felt like a thief as she clattered down the stone stairs in her new strappy sandals, and found her way along the corridor to the lounge she had passed on her way in.

She drifted across to the French windows at the far end of the room, which also stood ajar, and looked out into a courtyard where there were wooden chairs and a table under the shade of a tree, and beyond, a tiny cottage half hidden by a drift of cypress trees. And even as she stood there, gazing out, there was the sound of a car's engine pulling up outside the house.

She stiffened. Julian Tarrant was strolling casually through a stone archway into the courtyard, hands dug into the pockets of his jeans, walking as if time were of no importance and next week would do. He wore a beige sweater, his silver-blond hair was lighter than ever, bleached by the sun, and his face, by contrast, had lost the ashen pallor she remembered and was healthily bronzed. He looked tanned, fit and outrageously attractive.

He did *not* look overly ecstatic to see her, and Frankie's confidence plummeted even lower. She thought, This is not going to work. We are going to be adversaries. He should not have asked me to come unless he were prepared to drop his prejudices and trust my judgement and my professionalism.

What did he have against her? That she was a woman? An unattached woman? Did he see her as a threat to his carefully guarded male existence . . . did he fear that she might become attracted to him . . . that he would have to fend her off?

She took a fierce grip on her nerves as he pushed open the French windows and came in.

'So you made it, Ms Somers,' he said in a slow, cultured drawl.

'How could I have failed to, armed with your excellent directions?' she rejoined acidly. 'It might have been preferable had you been here when I arrived, or is it a custom of the country for the host to be absent when guests arrive?'

He returned her gaze dispassionately, quite untroubled by her outburst, and totally unashamed.

'It's a custom of mine to go walking in the hills as and when I feel the need to,' he replied. 'Since I had no way of knowing the exact time of your arrival, it would have been pointless for me to sit around here waiting. You're a grown-up girl, Ms Somers, and you weren't left sitting on the doorstep.'

He was talking logic, she was talking courtesy and consideration, and it was blindingly obvious to Frankie that they were not even speaking the same language! Furthermore, from the way he was looking at her, she knew that the cream dress had been a mistake. He was not impressed. He thought she was overdressed for the occasion, and out to try and upstage him with her city chic. His cool stare robbed her of whatever boost her clothes had given her. The ephemera of fashion did not concern him. This man saw through her, and he did not care for what he saw.

'You need not have dressed for dinner, either,' he said with mild sarcasm. 'As it happens, I have invited some friends over, but we are all very casual out here. Ah— if I am not mistaken, that sounds like them now.'

Frankie's nerves were so ragged with antagonism that she was almost relieved at the sight of the two complete strangers who had just appeared in the courtyard. The woman, in her late thirties, wore a cotton blouse and skirt and sandals, her reddish-gold hair dishevelled but her blue eyes friendly, with laughter-lines crinkling their corners. Her partner was a tall, rangy man in jeans and a cotton sweater, deeply sunburned, light brown hair receding from a high, reddened forehead. He was carrying a small barrel, she a large earthenware casserole dish partly covered by a cloth.

'I'm so sorry we're late, Julian, old thing,' the man said. 'That wretched pick-up of ours refused to start, and I've spent half the afternoon coaxing it back to life. I feel dreadful, after we promised to be here in case your editor arrived while you were out, but I hope you'll forgive us when you taste the splendid *coq au vin* that Jan's made for dinner.'

'These are two of my oldest friends, Noel and Jan Howerth,' Julian said. 'Jan, Noel—this is my editor, Ms Francesca Somers, who prefers to be known as Frankie.'

Frankie was still floundering, left nonplussed by the realisation that it was not, strictly speaking, Julian's fault that she had arrived to find the house empty. But he could have explained, she argued angrily with herself, instead of being so high and mighty about it, and then she need not have made embarrassing remarks about his lack of manners!

But it was impossible for her to withdraw what she had said, or even to allude to it, as Noel Howerth was already gripping her hand in his brown, slightly calloused one.

'Pleased to meet you. Can't see what old Caesar has done to merit the attentions of such a damned smart female,' he said with frank admiration. 'I thought editors were all crusty old blokes with horn-rimmed specs!'

'Take no notice of him, please,' his wife said, setting down the casserole on the table. 'He's been out in the sun too long, working in the olive groves. Those are ours you can see across the fields, although you can't quite see our house from here.'

Frankie smiled. 'But why did you say ''Caesar'' just now?' she asked curiously, rescuing her hand from Noel's fierce grasp.

He grinned. 'It's what we used to call Julian at school. We were there together, although I was a couple of years ahead. 'Well, his name was near enough to Julius, and he was obviously going to be a leader of men.' He hoisted the barrel on to the table. 'Get some glasses out, old boy. This is only plonk from the local co-operative, but it's very drinkable.'

Jan and Noel had not so much come to dinner as brought it with them. With the *coq au vin* there were early courgettes, carrots and new potatoes and a crusty loaf of home-baked bread. The wine they drank was the same robust country vintage as that in which the fowl had been cooked.

With the sun going down, the evening had begun to grow a little chilly, and Julian had closed the French windows. But the old walls of the house still retained the day's warmth, and there was no need for him to light the fire that was laid ready in the hearth.

They sat round a scrubbed pine table drawn up to the window, from where they could look out on an incredible night sky, velvet-clear and ablaze with stars. Julian Tarrant was on Frankie's left. He had pushed up the sleeves of his sweater above his elbows, and his arms were even more bronzed than his face, a deep golden colour. She was acutely aware of his hand nearest to her as it broke bread or lifted his wine glass, and it was with difficulty that she made herself meet his eyes when she spoke to him. When she did, she encountered no warmth in them, although he displayed plenty to his friends, with whom he shared an easy, jocular relationship.

Since he did not seem inclined to make conversation with her, Frankie did not force the issue, and talked mostly to Jan and Noel. She learned that he had given up a job in the city to live out here, cultivating their own fruit and vegetables and learning how to keep themselves. Jan had a small craft workshop where she made jewellery and pottery to augment their income, and they were clearly contented with the unconventional lifestyle they had chosen.

'It's worth the struggle,' Noel said. 'I dare say it's still cold and raining in London, and people are rushing about, pushing and shoving one another all over the place. How do you stand it?'

Frankie smiled. 'I sometimes wonder myself. But I love my job, and London is where the publishing world has its being. I have to admit, though, your way of life does have its attractions.'

'It's a little uncertain,' Jan said. 'But Noel and I were free to take the risk, as we have only ourselves to consider.' Her face clouded a little. 'We never had children, unfortunately. That would have made a difference.'

Beside her, Frankie heard Julian shift restlessly and saw his hand clench, savagely crumbling a piece of bread.

'Perhaps you should look on it rather as a problem you were spared,' he said, his voice dry, but tinged with bitterness.

Jan reached out and laid a hand on his arm, a sympathetic gesture Frankie would not have dared to make. She must have felt entitled to do so, in view of their long friendship, since he did not rebuff her. Obviously he was quite prepared to accept some women as friends... but not me, Frankie thought soberly.

'You mustn't give up, Julian. It will all work out, I know it,' Jan was saying quietly.

He smiled at her—that wonderful, grave but blinding smile which redrew the map of his face and invited exploration of the man behind it. He had only smiled once at Frankie that way. Perhaps it had been a mistake on his part, but she had not forgotten it.

'You are probably right,' he said, deliberately casting off gloom, or, what was more likely, withdrawing his private problems into his mental inner sanctum, where even his closest friends might hesitate to follow. He held out his glass. 'Let's have some more of this rot-gut of yours, Pongo.'

'Pongo?' Frankie exclaimed involuntarily.

'That's what they used to call *me* at school,' Noel admitted ruefully, and Frankie shook her head, laughing.

'I daren't ask why!'

'It had nothing to do with his personal bathing habits,' Julian said, and for the first time tonight, Frankie discerned a twinkle in the depths of the blue eyes. 'He used to smoke cigars, which was against the rules, of course, so he had to find hiding places, like cupboards under stairs, or inside the vaulting block in the gym. But then out would come these telltale clouds of pungent blue smoke...hence Pongo.'

His face had come alive with nostalgic humour as he told the story, and it occurred to Frankie that he was probably, when he chose to be so, a very entertaining man, with a lively, subversive wit. Somewhere inside the straight arrow, was there a closet hell-raiser who came out only occasionally, but with devastating results?

Jan was grinning. 'They're worse than a couple of adolescent boys once they get going on these reminiscences. Another few glasses of wine and they'll be singing the school song...with a few verses which weren't in the original version!'

'I would imagine that Frankie is broad-minded enough to handle it,' Julian said unexpectedly. 'We wouldn't make her blush.'

Frankie was startled, both by the remark and by the fact that he appeared to have decided to use her first name.

'You are not in a position to know that,' she responded swiftly. 'I might be as puritanical as a Victorian schoolmistress.'

'You might. But I doubt it,' he said levelly.

She did not blush, but knew a moment's strong fear that she would, as she forced herself to hold his gaze. What was he implying? Just because she had once said, only half seriously, that it would not have worried her to spend the night under his roof, it did not mean that she had expected to spend it in his bed, or that her philosophy of life was based on an easy morality. And oddly enough, only at that minute did the thought surface in her conscious mind that tonight she would indeed be sleeping under his roof. Well, if he thought she might be tempted to chase him around the bedposts, he was very severely mistaken!

'I think you presume far too much on too slight evidence,' she said coolly.

He shrugged. 'Not at all. I'm used to being in situations where my judgement of men has to be accurate and instantaneous.'

'Men, yes. I won't question your expertise there. But I happen to be a woman,' Frankie pointed out tartly.

Noel Howerth burst into appreciative laughter and lit up a Gauloise. 'I think she has you there, Julian, old son,' he grunted.

Julian Tarrant smiled, but it was a reserved, thoughtful, icy smile which warned Frankie that this man had an inbuilt resistance to losing anything... that the will to win was a vital component of his nature. She was sure he had been an excellent leader, and equally sure he would make an implacable and determined opponent.

But did their relationship *have* to be a struggle for supremacy? Was there not a level on which they could co-exist? Why was he so insistent on maintaining the upper hand, as if, should he give her an inch, her devious feminine ploys would immediately take a mile?

I'm fighting him because, in spite of everything, he attracts me, she admitted reluctantly, and I daren't allow myself to give in to it. Was he fighting her because his male instinct had, if only subconsciously, recognised this and determined to resist it? Frankie grew hot under the collar at the mere idea that he might have guessed at her unwilling susceptibility. She had to disabuse him of any such notion; she had to squash said feelings, firmly and unequivocally.

I do not need his approval, and if he thinks he is in any kind of danger from me he has seriously overestimated himself, she decided firmly. She would roast in hell before she would let him get to her!

Oddly enough, she was already beginning to feel dangerously warm.

CHAPTER FOUR

JAN was determined to wash up after dinner, and Frankie insisted on helping her, if only to escape, briefly, from a room with Julian Tarrant in it. She liked Jan, and considered that Julian probably had nicer friends than he deserved. Yet his association with Noel was an old, old friendship which had endured since schooldays. Noel must know Julian as well as anyone could, and was still here for him when needed. That must signify something, but Frankie was not sure what.

'This place is all still a bit haphazard,' Jan said apologetically as she stacked the dirty dishes in the old enamel sink. 'We bought it along with the rest of the property, and when we have done it up we shall probably let it commercially. Right now, it's only OK for Julian, who is used to roughing it. I hope you don't find it too primitive. Julian said you were a tough lady who wouldn't expect luxury.'

Did he, indeed? thought the tough lady, wondering just what else Julian had told his friends about her, and deciding firmly that it didn't matter to her if he had also said she was fat, frowsy and over the hill!

'Don't worry about me,' she said. 'Actually, I think the house is charming. I'm more concerned about Julian. With respect, he's not the easiest man to get along with.'

Jan's eyes softened.

'He's a touch raw around the edges at the moment,' she explained quietly. 'He's had a rough time—really rough, what with . . . well, it's for him to tell you about, if he chooses to. He tends to guard his inner self very closely.'

'I'd noticed,' Frankie said. 'But if I am to be any use to him as an editor I need to know him a little better. And it might have been less problematic if he had stayed in England.'

Jan merely smiled, accepting the criticism, but saying gently, 'Julian is here for his health, Frankie. He sustained a gunshot wound in Amazonia, and came back so badly injured that initially there were doubts he'd walk again. He recovered, thanks to excellent doctors and a will so fierce as to be frightening. But he still has quite a lot of pain at times, and the cold and damp exacerbate it.'

The brief curriculum vitae and the smattering of Press cuttings Frankie had read had told her virtually nothing of this. There had been no indication of the nature or extent of these injuries. She felt suddenly humbled, and could have kicked herself for her own insensitivity.

'I hadn't realised that,' she admitted.

'Well, it's unlikely that Julian will talk about it,' Jan said bluntly. 'He has said very little to anyone so far, and he's adept at keeping his own counsel about anything that matters to him personally. Noel and I love him to death, but I could slap him sometimes for that prickly pride of his.'

Frankie picked up a teatowel and began to dry plates furiously. Injury or no injury, she was not going to allow herself to be too impressed by Julian Tarrant. He would not have got himself hurt if he had not been playing cowboys and Indians in foreign parts, and she did not approve of that sort of adventure.

The evening ended with two cups each of excellent coffee, and then Jan and Noel began to make a move to leave. Frankie watched them go with a finely controlled but rising nervousness, and as Julian went out to see them off she busied herself with washing the coffee cups.

She heard him come into the kitchen, and, aware that he was standing behind her only an arm's length away, she almost let the last cup slip from her hand as she set it on the draining board.

'I'm aware that this must seem fearfully early to a city dweller like yourself, but we country people don't stay up late, either here or in England,' he said in a tone that was dry and languid, but to Frankie, full of insinuations she did not care for.

She turned to face him, drying her hands on the teatowel.

'Just because I live in London, it doesn't mean I'm out clubbing until dawn,' she retorted acidly. 'I'm a working woman, and that means of necessity an early riser, so I'm usually in bed by eleven, more often than not reading someone's manuscript.'

His enigmatic glance seemed to indicate that he thought it more likely she was curled up with a lover.

'Goodness—I had no idea your life was so dull and circumscribed, Frankie,' he said with mild sarcasm.

'It is, and what's more, that's just the way I like it,' she said firmly.

He shrugged. 'Then I won't ask you to share a nightcap with me,' he said, and the lack of regret in his voice told her that he'd had no intention of doing so anyhow. 'I prefer to start work early too. I use the cottage across the courtyard as a study, so I shall expect you there by eight-thirty prompt.'

It was obvious to Frankie that this was not in any way a suggestion, nor even a polite request. It was a command.

'Yes, sir,' she said, mock-subserviently. 'Just so long as you have coffee on the boil, because my brain cells don't function in the morning without it.'

Very briefly, she thought she glimpsed an amused challenge snapping in those amazing blue eyes. But she dared not look too closely as she passed him in the doorway with only inches to spare.

For all the tiring nature of the day, there was no hope of immediate sleep for Frankie as she lay in the dark in her narrow bed. Julian Tarrant was downstairs; very soon he would come up to bed, and he and she would be alone in this house in the wilds of the Languedoc, alone in the velvet night. What if he were to come into her room... what if he were to touch her...?

He wouldn't. He wasn't attracted to her, she told herself, and still was not sure if what she felt were relief or disappointment. Sleep still had not claimed her when she heard his firm footsteps climbing the stairs. A floor-board creaked as he passed her room, and she trembled slightly, her throat dry, the palms of her hands suddenly damp. Then she heard a door open and close further along the landing, and a little later the creak of bedsprings. She imagined him lying in bed, the powerful muscles of his shoulders and chest, naked...what would it be like to lie beside him...?

The house was silent. The night was silent. Alone with her crazy, unwelcome fantasies, Frankie sought the elusive release of sleep for a long time before it finally came to her.

She had set her travel alarm clock, determined that there was no way she was going to oversleep the next morning, but she did not need any artificial aids to wake her up. In the still, clear air birds were singing, and she opened her shutters to a pure blue and gold day, with an early promise of warmth to come.

Her night had been disturbed and uneasy, full of strange dreams, and now, in the light of day, she was ashamed of these nocturnal ramblings and anxious to get on with the task ahead of her. In plain language, her engine was running, and the knowledge that it was not going to be easy did not induce in her a desire to skulk beneath the duvet for as long as possible and wish the job in hand would go away. What could not be avoided she preferred to tackle head on, and quickly.

There was no sign of Julian in the house as she showered and put on jeans and a T-shirt, and pulled her hairbrush vigorously through her blonde crop. She wore no make up beyond a slick of lip gloss, but at the last moment she gave herself a swift spray of perfume, the only ego-boosting concession she allowed herself this morning.

The kitchen was empty, too. Frankie stepped out into the warm, glorious morning, feeling a momentary guilt on account of all those poor souls still shivering back at home. Then she reminded herself that she had Julian Tarrant to contend with, and *she* shivered. Every silver lining had a cloud! She forced a nonchalant shrug, and with pen and notebook folder tucked under her arm set off firmly across the courtyard to the cottage.

Close to, it looked smaller than ever, and possibly even older than the house. She saw no sign of life, but before she had even had time to rap on the door it was swiftly opened from within.

Julian Tarrant filled the frame of the doorway, and she was reminded forcefully once again of the size and power of him. He wore jeans and a short-sleeved shirt, and Frankie tried hard to ignore the flat stomach and fine shoulders, the muscles of his brown arms, the clean shaven jaw and the silvery glint of freshly washed hair. Without any overt effort, he made as clear a statement of calm and complete masculinity as she was going to read anywhere. Frankie had dealt skilfully with bottom-pinchers, wandering-handers and suggestive Romeos with bedroom eyes over the years, and none of them had thrown her like this man, who wasn't even trying, and did not particularly like her. It was violently unfair.

'Come in,' he said formally, leading her into the tiny room where he worked, which looked out over more olive groves, and a sun-browned vista of mountains undulating into a wild distance.

She could see he was already at work, in the orderly fashion she would have expected of him. Pads of lined paper neatly stacked, a shelf of reference books in strict alphabetical order, pens, pencils waiting in line, maps pinned up on the wall where he could see them easily. Frankie thought it was all just a bit too organised, too tidy. She had never met a writer who hadn't generated a certain chaos as part of the creative process.

He waved her to a seat opposite him at the table and, still standing, poured coffee from an enamelware pot.

She watched him spoon sugar into his, and then, his nose wrinkling in distaste, he said, 'Good lord, what are you wearing? One can smell it a mile away.'

'It's perfume, of course,' Frankie said, startled by his direct and uncompromising rudeness. 'No one has ever objected to it before—on the contrary. It's very expensive,' she added defensively.

'Oh, I'm sure,' he said drily. 'My wife used to drench herself in something she swore cost the price of a second mortgage, and which reminded me of tractor fuel.'

'I wear this perfume all the time. I'm surprised you haven't noticed it until now, and I'm afraid you'll just have to get used to it,' Frankie said curtly. 'Open a window or something.'

It was only the second time he had mentioned the former Mrs Tarrant to her, and he had, Frankie noted, forgotten to add the 'ex'. She wanted to say, Most women wear perfume, and whatever your wife did to you that's left you so bitter, I'm not guilty by association. But she thought these were troubled enough waters without her stirring them, so she left the words unspoken.

Sipping the ferociously strong coffee, she merely said, 'Perhaps I could read through chapter four while you press on with what you are doing. Then I'll have an idea of how it fits in with what you have written so far.'

'Sounds reasonable,' he agreed laconically, and as that seemed to be the extent of their communication Frankie made a start, and was soon deep in a description of a trek in the remote forests of New Guinea. Every now and then, as she paused to make a brief note, or scribble a longer comment in the margin of her pad, she could not resist glancing quickly and covertly at her companion. He was not, she observed, working with any great speed or fluency. Most of the time, in fact, he was gazing through the window into the middle distance, as if seeing not what was out there, but something else entirely. His brow was drawn into deep furrows, his lips were tightly compressed, and occasionally he tapped the table-top absently with the end of his pen.

Frankie was only too well aware that even the most experienced and committed of writers had days when it didn't flow, but she sensed a deeper malaise at work here, and it tied up with what she herself was reading. There was something missing.

All at once, he turned his head, looked across the table, and caught her studying him.

'What is it?' he said, with sharp percipience. 'If you have something on your mind, why don't you come right out and say it?'

Frankie moistened her lips with her tongue and took a deep breath.

'Very well. It's this. I just wonder sometimes . . . why are you writing this book?'

He regarded her steadily and then, quite dispassionately, with no hint of accusation in his voice, he said, 'Are you trying to tell me that it isn't any good?'

'No, I'm not,' she denied firmly. 'If I had thought that, I would have told you long before now. You clearly know your stuff, and you write with great style . . . but I don't sense any real commitment in you.' She paused, and as he remained silent went on carefully, 'Where writing is concerned, I usually advise if you don't want to do it above all, you would be better off doing something else.'

Julian Tarrant scraped back his chair and stood up, towering over her. A bitter, caustic, restless anger flowed from him, filling the air, enveloping everything in the room, himself and her included.

'*Like what*?' he demanded fiercely. He turned his back on her and stared out of the window, arms folded, and then, turning back, dug his hands deep into the pockets of his jeans. 'Like what?' he repeated, more bleakly, the anger gone, and a note almost of entreaty audible in his voice.

'Well . . . I don't know,' Frankie faltered, taken aback by the unsuspected force of emotion in him. 'How should I? I hardly know you. Plan another expedition, perhaps? Weren't you a little precipitate in announcing you were giving it up, when it has been your life for so long?'

'You think so?' he retorted dismissively. Then he sighed, as if the confession hurt him, and said, 'I didn't really have any choice. I'm not fit for that sort of activity any more, and probably never will be. Oh, I may seem it to you, and for everyday life I'm fine, but believe me, I know the difference. I would never be one hundred per cent sure of myself, and when your own life and the lives of others might depend on your stamina, or the speed of your reactions in a dangerous situation, ninety nine per cent is not enough. That life is over for me, Frankie, whether I like it or not.'

Silently, she poured some more coffee. It was tepid, but he didn't seem to care, and neither did she. She was shaken by the profundity of his revelation of the great, yawning gap in his life he was desperately trying to fill, plugging away at the emptiness with ferocious mental effort.

He leaned back against the window, large hand folded around the coffee mug, chest rising and falling with a steady, discernible rhythm.

'I suppose I could always go back to Cerne Farm and sit in my empty house, making phone calls to my children who, so I am always told, are not there at the time I ring,' he said sardonically. 'Failing that, I could take my shotgun and blow my bloody brains out. I choose to do this instead. So do I have your professional permission to push on?'

'Of course,' Frankie said quietly, but there was a tremor in her voice she could scarcely suppress. Her measured comment had opened up a Pandora's box of anger and emotion and sheer despair, and she wasn't sure it was within her power…or her mandate…to cope with it. 'I'm so sorry, Julian. I didn't realise.'

She forced an artificially bright smile. 'Tell me about your children. How old are they?'

He was calm, now, perfectly controlled, as though the outburst had never taken place.

'Jeremy is fifteen, Karin is twelve. They are both with my ex-wife. I hardly ever see them, and whenever I do, they seem to have changed out of all recognition.'

'That happens. I'm told it's normal,' Frankie said steadily, conversationally. 'Of course, I'm not a mother, but lots of my friends have children who treat me as a kind of honorary aunt. The teenage years are not easy.'

He smiled, the hollow appeared at the side of his jaw, and some of the ice in his eyes thawed. She saw he understood very well what she was trying to do.

'It's all right, Frankie,' he said, quite gently. 'I don't require a shrink—just an editor. I wonder—would it be fearfully sexist of me if I asked you to make some fresh coffee?'

'Not at all,' she said promptly. Not if he put it like that. And when he smiled that way it was enough to persuade anyone to walk barefoot over hot coals, if it would make him happy.

She worked on for the rest of the morning, suppressing her slight unease. Whatever was eating away at Julian Tarrant from within was not really her province. She worked for Cooper Masterman, and her only brief was to encourage him to write the best book he was capable of writing. Did she need to know his reasons? She was not a therapist. Professional interest was one thing; too deep an involvement was quite another. She had never before had the slightest difficulty in distinguishing one from the other, so what in the world was happening now?

She was still wrestling with this dilemma when he suggested that they break for lunch. They ate outside at the table under the trees, more of Jan's home-baked bread which she had brought over the previous evening, and cheese from Noel's goats.

Opening a bottle of *eau minerale*, he said, 'What I told you this morning is strictly between ourselves. It isn't for general chat around your office when you get back to London.'

Frankie gasped. She'd had no intention of discussing with anyone what he had told her, which anyhow was little enough, and she was both hurt and angry that he thought she would indulge in that sort of gossip.

'I don't discuss my authors' problems or their private confidences with other people, either in or out of the office!' she declared hotly, meeting the hard blue challenge in his eyes head on. 'I do have to phone my office, but I can assure you it won't be to talk about you. I have other things on my plate, and I have to make sure nothing untoward has happened in my absence. You can believe that or not, as it suits you.'

He continued to hold her gaze, but his shoulders rose and fell in a slight shrug.

'As you wish, but you will have a long drive to the telephone. The nearest one is outside the Bureau de Poste in the village you must have passed on the way here.'

'But that's miles away!' Frankie gasped. 'Don't you have one in the house?'

'No, and neither do Jan and Noel. Bliss, isn't it?' Julian said drily, favouring Frankie with an oblique, sardonic smile which said plainly that he expected an urban female like herself to start experiencing immediate withdrawal symptoms.

'Not if there were a genuine emergency, it wouldn't be!' she snapped back at him.

'I can cope with most emergencies myself, Frankie, so what did you have in mind?' he taunted her with a grin. Feigning a frown, he said, 'Ah…I get it! You mean, like running short of perfume, that sort of thing?'

Exasperation welled up in her to the point where she began to doubt she could contain it, and she jumped up, hoping vainly that movement would dissipate her anger.

'No, of course not! Stop trying to make out I'm some stupid, brainless female who is hooked on trivia!' she exclaimed. 'You know damn well it's not true! Just think for a minute, Julian—what would happen if one of us had some sort of accident, marooned out here, miles from any sort of help. It could happen. Even you are not invincible.'

He rose, too, standing so close that she could feel his body heat.

'What kind of accident did you have in mind, Frankie?' he drawled. 'Is one of us about to do the other an injury? No doubt I should be shaking in my shoes, as I am already walking wounded, and you are a formidable woman.'

It was so patently obvious that he could have floored her in one move if he'd had half a mind to. But he had an Achilles' heel that she had discovered that morning, and in her fury, she did not hesitate to play on this vulnerability.

'I know this may be a difficult concept for you to grasp, but some of us have people back home who actually *want* us to keep in touch with them!' she flung at him.

The minute the remark left her lips, she recognised it for what it was, a mean, hurtful blow aimed completely below the belt. He took a step back from her, without haste, withdrawing into the inaccessible fastness of his own pain, and Frankie shrivelled inwardly beneath the cold lash of his contemptuous blue glare.

'Please yourself what you do, and whom you contact,' he said shortly. 'I shan't be around this afternoon. I'm going out walking—somewhere where the air is a bit cleaner.'

Frankie wanted desperately to say, 'I'm sorry, that was small-minded of me, and I should not have said it.' But the words stuck in her throat. She could not, dared not, put herself in such a position of abject surrender where this man was concerned, because the minute she stopped detesting his arrogance and permitted a whisper of sympathy to sneak into her feelings for him, she was afraid she would leave herself wide open, exposed to... to who knew what else? She could not afford the weakness an apology would reveal.

So instead she said irritably, 'It's all very well for you to stomp off whenever anyone happens to say something that annoys you, but I didn't come all this way to sit twiddling my thumbs! I want to get on with some work.'

'There's nothing to stop you,' he said with distant unconcern. 'Wait there.'

He disappeared into the cottage, returning a moment later with a pile of manuscript in his hands, which he slapped down on the table in front of her. 'Enough to keep you going, I trust,' he said, and then he turned, went back into the cottage and slammed the door.

Frankie was so disturbed that she could not immediately settle down to work. Instead, she drove down to the village and phoned her office from the booth outside the *poste*.

Sally reassured her that all was well, and that there had been no alarms in her absence.

'How is it with the great he-man?' she asked curiously. 'Are you enjoying your visit?'

'That's not exactly the word I would use,' Frankie demurred. She was in no mood and no state to talk about Julian at the moment. Moving on to other matters, she gave Sally instructions concerning several things she wanted her to deal with. Putting down the receiver, she was almost overcome by a sudden fierce desire to be back home, among people who knew her, going to the office every day, doing familiar things. Safe. Unthreatened. Not standing in a sunlit square in the Languedoc, torn by strange emotions, her life caught up and tangled, however briefly, with Julian Tarrant's.

In this confused state, she emerged from the phone booth and ran full tilt into Jan, who had her shopping basket over her arm.

'Well, hello again,' she said cheerily. 'How's it going? I would have expected you to be hard at work.'

Frankie sighed. She had specifically told Julian she did not gossip, but she needed help to understand him if they were to work together at all. Surely it was all right to talk to Jan, who knew him so well?

'I think I've trodden on Julian's toes,' she said rue-fully. 'I said something he didn't like, and he stalked off in a huff. I wouldn't blame you for thinking I'm making a pig's ear of this.'

'Come and have a coffee,' Jan said, drawing Frankie across to the village's one small bar which had a few rickety tables outside on the pavement. After she had ordered, she said, 'Maybe it wouldn't do Julian any harm to get good and angry. He's been too bottled up for too long. Somehow, he has to let it all out if he's to make sense of the rest of his life. And he has so much still to give—so much strength and quality and unused po-tential. It mustn't go to waste.'

'It isn't that I want to pry,' Frankie insisted. 'But... I can't open my mouth without putting my foot in it. He admits he misses the call of the wild, and that his mar-riage broke down. That's all. I feel it's only part of the picture.'

Jan stared down into her coffee.

'I don't know an awful lot myself,' she confessed. 'It's more what Noel and I have pieced together from odd remarks than what Julian has actually told us. But you are right. Your ignorance of the facts isn't going to help either of you.'

She paused briefly. 'Somewhere in the wild, border regions of Amazonia, Julian's expedition strayed into an area of fighting between guerrilla factions. It turned out nastier than could have been envisaged. I honestly don't know the details, only that he got all his people safely out of it, but at great cost to himself. He was nearly killed—in fact, his life hung in the balance for some days. The doctors put him together again, miraculously, but he knows he will never again be fit for that kind of thing. He's a restless, outdoor man, a man of action, and I don't think his suffering is purely physical. There's something else... it's not easy to do a complete re-think of your future in such circumstances.'

'I'm sure it isn't,' Frankie said cautiously. There was more to come, she knew, but she dared not prompt. Her own throat was dry, the skin of her palms prickled painfully.

'With the strength of will he has, and given a good, secure family background, a loving wife, he'd have made it,' Jan said. 'Unfortunately, Julian didn't have a loving wife to support him. He came back physically and mentally wrecked, only to find that Alison had been sleeping with another man.'

A long, cold shudder ran down Frankie's back. 'She left him?' she finished. 'At a time like that, she just deserted him?'

Jan gave a sad, rueful little shrug. 'As I told you, I don't know the whole story. But, knowing Julian, I would imagine that as soon as he had the strength he threw her out, bag and baggage! But she held a trump card. She took the children with her. Not content with that, she's doing everything in her power to poison them against him and keep him from them.'

Driving back up the lonely road to the house faster than she should have, Frankie mulled over what Jan had told her.

Alison. She had a name now—she was real, this woman who had lived with Julian for long enough to be the mother of his fifteen-year-old son. He must have loved her very much to be so gutted by her ill-timed desertion.

Who was she fooling with that past tense? He still loves her, she told herself grimly. She had broken up his home, taken his children from him, had an affair with another man, and he was still so totally destroyed by it all that no other woman could mean a thing to him.

She revved the engine savagely as she tore round a bend. *There is nothing you can do about it, Frankie.* Except help him with this book. If he saw her as a woman at all, it was only as a representative of a species he mistrusted violently.

More by luck than by judgement, she reached the house safely, but as she jerked viciously on the handbrake this furious dialogue with herself still raged on. I don't *want* him to see me as a woman. The hell you don't!

Slamming the car door behind her, she stormed indoors.

CHAPTER FIVE

THE house was silent and empty. Frankie took Julian's manuscript outside and, sitting at the table, with the sun filtering down through the leaves of the trees, forcibly blotted out everything from her mind except her vital critical response to what she was reading. It wasn't easy, and only years of practice enabled her to channel her concentration in denial of the turmoil inside her.

An hour or so into this and she came to a point where something obviously did not run on as it should, and, glancing at the page numbering, she at once saw why. There appeared to be several pages missing.

She could have read on and returned to the missing piece later, when he gave it to her, but it came at a particularly crucial point, and she disliked losing the flow and continuity of the whole. The pages could only be on the table where he had been working that morning. It was always unwise to predict what would annoy or anger Julian, but she could see no logical reason why he should object to her retrieving them.

She shrugged and rose to her feet decisively, brushing her hands down the sides of her jeans as if the gesture could as easily brush off her uncertainty. He was already so displeased with her that it was difficult to see how she could make matters worse.

The cottage door was predictably unlocked, so she pushed it open and went into the cramped little room. Everything seemed to be just as he had left it before they broke off for lunch, and surely the missing pages must be right here on the table, next to the chapter he was currently writing.

Either pure chance or habit made her glance down at the open notebook in front of her. Either way it was fatal, for after that one glance, her unassailable editorial senses were engaged, and there was no way she could have turned her eyes away from what she had begun to read.

For this was not Julian Tarrant's careful, skilfully written account of his expeditions. This was something else...something so immediate and personal that it leapt from the page and grabbed her by the throat. It was the same handwriting and the same voice, but this was Julian's unique account of his own life. Almost holding her breath, Frankie slid into his chair and read on, unable to resist turning the pages.

She went with him to university, learning, to her surprise, what should not have surprised her—that his degree was in anthropology, the source of an abiding interest in the natural world. She endured with him the hardships of survival training, the acquisition of skills and techniques which would stand him in good stead in the years to come. She accompanied him on his first lone forays into desolate places, mourned with him when he inherited Cerne Farm on the death of his father.

She knew, glimpsing briefly ahead, that the accounts of his expeditions as detailed here would be written from an entirely different angle, not scientific, but personal, and realised, with a quickening of the pulse, that if she only read on far enough, this journal would tell her in depth about the dramatic incident in the jungles of Amazonia which had put an end to his career. For this was not, to use her own derogatory expression, *Boys' Own Paper* stuff. It was the real and thoughtful testament of an intelligent and sensitive man, full of his own thoughts, his own philosophy, his doubts and reservations, honest enough to admit to the dark places of his own psyche...as here, where he lamented man's ruination of his planet, and feared for his own part in it. The words he chose to describe this loss of innocence were not his own, but those of William Wordsworth, expressing the same fears almost two centuries earlier...

> For I have learned to look on nature not as in the hour
> Of thoughtless youth; but hearing oftentimes
> The still, sad music of humanity...

Frankie sat riveted to her seat. Painful fingers gnarled around her heart, and squeezed hard. She knew, with the instinct of her trade which she trusted implicitly, that she was reading a small masterpiece. She knew, too, that five minutes of such reading had revealed to her more of Julian Tarrant than he had ever told her...or ever would, most likely. And she was able to identify, now, the missing element which had troubled her this morning. It was here. He was writing this because he *had* to. It was as simple as that.

'What the hell do you think you are doing in here?'

His voice was terrifying in its cold, level, furious displeasure. Frankie looked up and turned her head, while the rest of her remained as motionless as granite, frozen in helpless immobility. His presence filled the room with a lethally controlled aggression, and in that moment, she was scared as no human being had ever scared her before.

'Get out,' he said, the arctic eyes fixed on her like lasers, brittle pinpoints of light glittering in their depths. The habit of unquestioned command reinforced his voice, and he had no need to raise it to make her feel the full weight of its authority.

But Frankie was not temperamentally inclined to obedience. The blood began to flow angrily back into her veins, and she reminded herself defiantly that he was only a man! One man! And she was not committing any crime.

'Keep your hair on,' she said bitingly. 'The manuscript you gave me had some pages missing, and I came to look for them. That's all.'

'I said—*get out*,' he repeated implacably. 'Did you hear me?'

He took one stride, seized both her wrists and hauled her unceremoniously to her feet. It cost him no effort whatsoever, and to her immense chagrin she discovered she could not break free from his grasp.

'For God's sake, Julian, stop this!' she gasped. 'If you will leave your door unlocked, and things lying open on your desk, what do you expect?'

'I *expect* my privacy to be respected,' he said, laying cold, heavy emphasis on the word. 'I do not expect to find anyone poking and prying among my personal effects, which are none of their concern. In short, Ms Somers, I *expect* you to mind your own damn business. Or is that entirely unreasonable of me?'

'How would you know what reasonable behaviour is?' she shot back at him. 'You haven't shown a shred of evidence of it since the day I met you! But then, that's exactly what *I* would expect from a man whose attitude towards women has succeeded in driving even his own wife away!'

It happened all in a second. Her insult, thrown at him in furious desperation, provoked a strange new light in his eyes, and he reacted with a swift, instinctive response, dragging her away from the table and whirling her round. Her arms buckled at the elbows, bringing her clenched hands, still pinioned at the wrists, up hard against his chest. She could feel him breathing, steadily and without any exertion, feel the rise and fall of his ribcage, while, inches away from hers, the lines of his face tautened, and the muscle jumped at the side of his jaw.

Her own breath was suspended in her throat, her chin tilted up combatively, her eyes refusing to evade his. The sudden outflow of tension from him, like the ebbing of a long-dammed tide, caught her in its backwash. Something unknown seized and shocked her as his mouth came down hard on hers. It ran amok, unchecked, the length of her body wherever it made contact with his, and it gave him back his fierce, ungentle kiss with an equal savagery.

Behind her head, the map on the wall rustled and tore as the weight and force of his body pressed her backwards. He continued to ravage her mouth until she was bruised and breathless, and she offered no denial, not even a pretence of protest. There was nothing he could do to her that she would not welcome at that moment, that she would not, on some dark, dimly understood level, take pleasure in.

It took only seconds before pride, sense and the remnants of her civilised self struggled to the surface through the red haze that had seized her, and in the same instant a similar impulse must have reasserted itself in him. He all but flung her from him, turning his back so that she was left staring at the stubborn breadth of his shoulders.

Frankie leaned her head back against the wall, taking deep breaths to recharge her lungs and steady the trembling in her legs. She had just looked down into a chasm of desire so deep that she could not fathom it—she, who had always prided herself that she was in control of her sexuality, and not it of her. She wanted to run, to get out, before he saw the weakness in her that he had brought about, but contrarily she could not. She had to confront him first, to regain some of the ground he had taken from her, so she stayed where she was, silent and unmoving, as he slowly turned to face her again.

She had expected his face to be cold and resentful, and she was therefore surprised by an expression on it that was almost wry, coming close to an admission that he had taken himself by storm almost as much as he had taken her.

'Well, now,' he said quietly, 'it has to be said, that's not the way in which I usually operate.'

A sharp, offended laugh escaped her.

'Naturally, it happens to me all the time!' she said sarcastically. 'Being set upon by angry authors is an occupational hazard I take in my stride! If that was an apology, I must say, I've heard better.'

'It wasn't,' he said bluntly. 'Maybe I was out of order. Well—all right, I'll admit that much. But you have deliberately goaded me and sniped at me since the day we met. You should have realised...indeed, I'm sure you are well aware that I am not a man to suffer such provocation.'

She gasped, winded with outrage.

'Provo...no, it's too much!' she declared. 'If, as you say, I've goaded you, it's only because you have incessantly tried to put me down and taunt me on account of my sex! That wasn't provocation, it was retaliation! And in any case, it doesn't give you the right to...to assault me!'

To her chagrined astonishment, he laughed outright.

'Come off it, Frankie! If you insist on equal rights, play fair! Had you really considered that you were being assaulted, you could have taken appropriate action...slapped my face, stamped on my foot...or whatever,' he drawled amusedly.

'I didn't have a whole lot of opportunity,' she protested, rubbing her aching wrists. 'You perhaps are not aware of your own strength. If you are on the sick list, I'm thankful I didn't meet you when you were in the peak of condition.'

The look she caught unawares in his eyes then drove home all too clearly the fact that had she met him in those days such a thing would never have happened. He would never have kissed her, or been galled into an impulse to do so. Then, he would have had Alison. He would have had future expeditions to plan, ambitions to fulfil...he would have been a complete and confident man.

He was right. She had fought him with her intellect, with her sharp wit, with the sly hint and the cutting, rebarbative comment, but the moment he had taken her in his arms her resistance had crumbled and she had not fought him at all. But he had been compelled more by anger than by desire...and maybe it had been some time since he had touched a woman at all, Frankie thought, remembering the ferocity of those kisses. The notion was thoroughly shaming, and it reduced her to the status of a mere vehicle for his lust.

He sighed, as if the whole business had all at once become too boring and unimportant for him to trouble himself further with.

'If you are saying that you don't want anything of that kind to happen again, then rest assured, it won't,' he stated firmly. 'If you want me to give you my word, I will, although I know you think I'm not to be relied on or trusted any more, and perhaps you are right. But there it is. Take it or leave it.'

Beneath the abruptness were untold layers of disappointment, disillusionment, the deep, resentful questioning of an unfair fate and the blows it had dealt him— *why me*? There was also a fierce, bitter, independent will to make it back alone, to ask for no man or woman's help, pity or understanding.

Julian Tarrant would survive. But was mere survival the best he could hope for? Was it anything like enough?

Frankie stayed on another full day, but not until the morning she was due to leave did she risk broaching the subject of the material she had inadvertently discovered on Julian's desk.

She sought him out in his study in the cottage, seated at his table working, a frown creasing his forehead. He looked up as she entered, taking in her neat, tailored dress and jacket, the flight bag slung over her shoulder.

'You're off, then?' he asked distantly, his voice devoid of emotion.

'Yes.' She kept her own demeanour equally detached. She had worked with him the previous day only by dint of avoiding completely any reference to what had happened before, and he had gone along with this punctiliously, behaving towards her with a cool, structured politeness she had returned in like measure. Both of them had known that this was the only way.

Impossible to pretend that it hadn't happened, that the violent, subterranean forces rumbling dangerously beneath the surface of their relationship had not briefly and explosively broken through. She could not forget those furious moments when he had brutally and forcefully kissed her...and she, far from objecting, had given him back in kind.

Since he had not mentioned it and, she was sure, would not do so, she would probably never know how he looked back on this episode. Most likely with the annoyance with which he regarded any lapse in his own tight self-control, she thought, not without a sense of shame. She was sure he did not recall it with any pleasure.

'I reckon you're well on course, now, but if you have any problems or queries you can always call me,' she said. 'Are you planning on spending any length of time here?'

'Planning?' He repeated the word as if it were alien to him. 'I have no idea, Frankie. That will depend on...many things.' He did not enlarge on what these might be, which made it very plain that his personal considerations were none of her concern. 'Well...have a good flight back,' he added, in a voice taut with dismissal.

Frankie hesitated, but only fractionally. She had been at the receiving end of Julian's wrath enough times not to underestimate its potency, but she simply could not walk away leaving unsaid what was occupying her mind with such strength and urgency.

'Julian.'

'Uh?' He looked up again. 'Hell, are you still here? Can't a man get on with his work?'

'Most certainly.' She inhaled deeply, as one taking a parachute jump with no assurance that the thing would open, let alone permit her a safe landing. 'But *which* work—that's the question.'

His eyes narrowed to dangerous slits, and she sensed him withdrawing into a guarded suspicion.

'The book you are engaged on is good. Although it won't make you rich, it will earn you some money and an increased scientific prestige. I don't think that you're desperate for either.'

He tapped the edge of the table with his pen in slow, rhythmic irritation, leaning back in his chair and regarding her from eyes that were half closed, but menacingly alert. 'Get to the point, please.'

'The point is, what you should be publishing are those personal memoirs you were so angry with me for reading,' she said, burning her boats and saying a short, silent prayer for her own safety.

Amazingly, he displayed no anger whatsoever. But he stopped tapping the table with his pen, and his very stillness was intimidating.

'You have got to be clean out of your mind,' he said, coldly and flatly. 'Those memoirs, as you call them, are nothing more than my private thoughts and recollections about my life and my experiences, and that's exactly what they will remain—private. They are not for publication, nor are they for anyone else to read. Forget you ever saw them—because you shouldn't have.'

She winced slightly.

'I know, but I did see them, and I can't just forget to order,' she said. 'Julian, what you have there is a brilliant piece of writing—unique, sad, funny, thoughtful—revealing. Something *you* can say, which no one else could. The commitment and the . . . the passion are all in there.'

A frozen, sardonic smile twisted his mouth.

'Passion is something you would know a lot about, I take it?' he queried caustically.

Frankie fought off the memory of his mouth bruising hers, the hard, powerful body crushing her against the wall, searing her with a fierce satisfaction. If he was hinting at a libidinous nature, he was way off beam, for although she considered herself to be perfectly normal, no man had ever made her burn with sensual hunger the way he had.

'I recognise it when it leaps out at me from the page in the form of the written word, yes,' she said tartly. 'I recognise it in a voice speaking clearly out of its own experience, and holding nothing back, even its doubts. You can't deny it, either, a man who can quote Wordsworth . . .'

He moved at last, rising swiftly to his feet and looking down at her, hands planted squarely on his hips.

'That bothers you, does it?' he demanded with dry disdain. 'Rough types shouldn't overreach their limitations by admitting to a knowledge of poetry, certainly not stuff like Wordsworth? Perhaps something a little more gung-ho would have fitted in more neatly with your inbuilt prejudices.'

'But I don't——' she began indignantly, and then stopped, because of course, he was right. She did. All along, from the very beginning, she'd had a preconceived notion of someone hard, tough and aggressive. Which he was. But he was also reflective, humourous, cultured…a loving father, a valued friend…a man who had trusted a woman, perhaps too implicitly for his own good.

She sighed and capitulated.

'All right, so I had you wrong—at least partly. You'll be telling me next that you grow flowers,' she said ruefully.

He smiled. The genuine, heart-thumping, thousand-watt smile.

'But I do,' he said. 'Roses, actually. Of course, neither the season nor the weather were right when you visited Cerne Farm. You must come down in summer and see it in all its true glory.'

Her own answering smile was tentative. Behind the embittered, defensive front he almost always presented to her, she glimpsed briefly the whole man he had once been, the kind of man a woman must surely have been off her head to leave. She wondered fleetingly what Alison Tarrant had found in someone else, to replace what she had thrown aside.

'I'd like to,' she said. 'But will you be there?'

'I expect so,' he said with a resigned sigh, crisping a hand through the glinting wave of his hair. 'It was good of Jan and Noel to lend me this place, but, attractive as the climate is, it isn't home. Nor can I expect to be granted the privilege of my children's company during the school holidays if I'm absent from the parental home, can I? Besides, Dorset in summer is a desirable place to be.'

She heard it, then. Clearly. Homesickness, longing, regret for a life that had passed. Her own heart turned over inside her with sadness, and without thinking, she reached out and laid a hand on his bronzed forearm.

Wanting to touch him, yes, but wanting also to offer the willing gift of human contact that said, I understand and I feel for you.

He shook off her hand as if she had burned him.

'Damn it, Frankie, I don't need your pity,' he said. 'I can feel sorry enough for myself.'

Stinging with rejection, she retorted, 'If you can't tell pity from a genuine offer of friendship, perhaps you're beyond help!'

'Perhaps I am,' he agreed readily. 'And I don't need you around reminding me of the fact. Go away, Frankie. You're too much woman.'

Her steady amber gaze engaged his. Was that a compliment or a condemnation? An acknowledgement that in a sense, he found her disturbing? Or merely a fervent desire to be done with her, to be left alone with his unworked-through grief?

'Okay, I'm going,' she said, forcing a grin. 'About that journal——'

'No. Absolutely not!' he cut her off, ice-cold and adamant in refusal. 'That journal is not for publication. And if you so much as mention it again, I'll——'

'You'll what?' she asked sweetly, unable to resist a final taunt. 'Have me beaten?'

He leaned back against the wall, arms folded, regarding her with a steady, forthright, peculiarly thoughtful stare.

'Oh, no, Frankie. Some tasks you don't delegate,' he said pleasantly. 'This one I'd do myself.'

With a snort of angry disdain, she turned and marched out. Don't try it! Don't even contemplate it, said her stiff back and erectly poised head. But she did not doubt for one minute that he was fully capable of carrying out the threat, and the uncomfortable awareness that beneath the surface indignation a fierce, unwilling excitement surged through her at the mere idea made her wonder about her own continued sanity.

Most of April saw Frankie so busy at work she scarcely had time to turn around. She had several projects coming up to the proof stage, racing against production schedules that had to be met; she was involved in liaising with Cooper Masterman's publicity department on promotions for forthcoming publications, and putting together artwork and text. Meanwhile, she still had to keep her various authors happy, dealing with their queries and soothing their anxieties.

She should have been relieved that Julian Tarrant did not seem to require anything more of her. Having ironed out the points that had caused him concern, he appeared to know exactly where he was headed, and apart from a short, terse note saying he expected to deliver his completed manuscript by September, as had been envisaged and planned for, she heard nothing from him.

So I have plenty to occupy my time, and I don't need brusque telephone calls from him, or peremptory instructions to jump on a plane to Toulouse and drop everything else, she argued with herself.

The time she had spent with him had been a deeply traumatic experience. Like him or not, she had been plagued by an obsessive desire to be taken in his arms. Her physical awareness of him had been so overwhelming as to be painful, and this had been so even when she had felt most strongly opposed to him, as much as in their rare moments of unexpected rapport.

She could do without that. How could she relate sex-ually to a man with whom she shared nothing, not even a basic commonality of ideas? She had fallen into bed and into marriage with Tom because she had imagined herself 'in love', but then she had been eighteen, and ignorant. She was not going to be bowled over by sexual attraction now that she was pushing thirty and knew better.

'There hasn't been any word from your hero,' Sally remarked one afternoon in the office as they were snatching a quick coffee break.

'If you mean Julian Tarrant, no, there hasn't. And I wouldn't exactly call him that,' she replied.

'I don't know. He has risked his life many times in dangerous places,' Sally mused. 'He must be very brave to do that. You have to admire his courage.'

'You really think so? That's a simplistic view,' Frankie snapped scathingly. 'The other side of that coin is a stubborn bloody-mindedness and a tendency to ag-gression. I fail to see what you find so admirable about that!'

Seeing Sally's surprised and wounded expression, Frankie sat back, and a small sigh escaped her. 'Oh, lord, Sally, I didn't mean to yell at you. I don't know why I've become so bitchy lately.'

'You aren't normally bitchy at all,' Sally said shrewdly, 'only when the subject of Julian Tarrant comes up. He has some sort of strange effect on you, but you won't admit it. Perhaps it's that he makes you feel like a woman.'

'I can assure you that I have never felt like anything else!' Frankie protested.

'You know what I mean. Like a woman—inside,' Sally persisted.

'What nonsense! Have you been reading those romantic serials in the magazines in the dentist's waiting-room?' Frankie laughed, trying to make light of it, but although Sally only pursed her lips, shook her head and said nothing more, Frankie knew that she didn't fool her.

She didn't do a very good job of fooling herself, either. Julian Tarrant did make her feel like a woman, but not in any way that was comfortable or that she was accustomed to. He stroked all her nerve-endings the wrong way, reminded her constantly of the female vulnerability of her own body. She suffered a vague, persistent ache for something she had never known and hitherto never wanted—a man strong enough, dominant enough to master her.

She met plenty of men both through work and socially, but none of them excited even a spark of interest in her. Somehow, they all seemed to her like…like boys, shallow and inexperienced in the hard lessons of life. They had not been through the fire and come back. They had not been tested to the limits of their endurance.

In short, they were not Julian Tarrant. Men like him did not grow on trees, they were not found around every street corner, or propping up the bar in every club. A grim desperation seized her as she realised that she was now comparing every man who crossed her path with him. Unfavourably.

She worried too about Julian's memoirs. She had said nothing to Ivor or to anyone else at Cooper Masterman about them, and even now she was unresolved in her mind about the ethics involved. Professionally speaking, when she had wind of anything so original and saleable, she supposed she should have done so. The company paid her and was entitled to her loyalty. Very well, so Julian had insisted he would not publish, but authors had said that before, and had been persuaded to think again.

Ivor, if he knew, would undoubtedly have put pressure on her to do something about it, which meant that she, in turn, would be expected to pressurise Julian. He was a formidable man to try and influence, as she knew only too well, but it was not only the prospect of his whiplash scorn and anger which deterred her.

Her reluctance went deeper than that. Much as she would have loved to bring this unique statement of personal experience to the light of print, she had felt in Julian a vulnerability, despite his deeply masculine strength. Much more than his body had been wounded, and the healing process had scarcely begun. The scars were still fresh, and if writing his journal helped to heal them she could not bear to sabotage this delicate and possibly vital process.

If she were thinking more as a woman than as an editor—and she *was*, she admitted soberly—then so be it. It could not be helped.

So she held her peace, deliberately, and then one morning in May, when the birds were trilling ecstatically in every London park, and the girls were blossoming out in their summer clothes, she walked into the reception area to find Sally waiting, regarding her with an expression of new interest and expectancy.

'You have a visitor in your office,' she said.

And there he was.

CHAPTER SIX

HE WORE a suit. That was the first thing she registered about him, for she had never seen him dressed with anything approaching formality before. It was a good suit of a fine, light wool, slate-grey, and he looked particularly distinguished in it, but she could not help viewing it as a disguise. The garb declared, 'I am just like any other man you might meet on the street,' but she knew it was not so. He was sailing under false colours, and it would be unwise to be deceived.

'This is an unexpected pleasure,' she said smoothly, taking great care to compose her face into its friendly/businesslike smile and extending a hand. Quite ridiculously, her knees were trembling, and she felt literally in shock. 'I do hope it doesn't mean you're encountering problems with your book.'

He took her hand. Held it for no more than a few seconds, but the touch of his hard, dry fingers set a mischievous pulse racing at her wrist, and waves of excitement leap-frogging up her arm. Damn him—it was still here! He could still do this to her. She had hoped it had been only a passing illusion.

'Not really,' he said. 'At least, none I can't solve myself. I had to be in England for a couple of days, so I thought I would take the opportunity to see where Cooper Masterman lived, moved and had their being.'

'It's a social call?' Frankie allowed just a touch of surprise to inflect her voice.

'A courtesy call.' The correction was slight, but she took the point. He had not sought her out personally, but had paid a visit to his publishing company, with whom she was his point of liaison. There was a fine but clear distinction, and she accepted it. Why should he want to see her? Most of their previous encounters had been fraught with disagreement and barely resolved conflict. But this realisation cast a cloud over the pleasure in seeing him there which had ambushed her so suddenly and completely that she was unable to deny it.

She opened the door a fraction and called out, 'Sally— could we have some coffee, please?' before sliding into the seat behind her desk. From this position she was once again Frankie Somers, editor, and this should have afforded her some security, some protection. But there was none. Julian Tarrant threatened, unnerved, disturbed and excited her no less because the width of the executive desk separated them, and the keen blue eyes, even more emphatic in the bronzed face, rested on her consideringly.

'How are Noel and Jan?' she asked politely, catching hold of what she hoped was a safe subject, although with this man one could never be entirely sure.

'Very well. They send their regards,' he replied, pausing as Sally set two cups in front of them.

'Sugar please, Sally,' Frankie said, and across the desk she saw Julian's smile twitch briefly, as if in recollection. Of what? The time spent together in his small study in the cottage? The afternoon when he had surprised her reading his journal, and reacted with such violence . . . when she had ended up in his arms?

She was obliged to look away, and that irked her deeply. Damn him, just because he had kissed her, did

the memory of it have to hang between them constantly?
And did *she* have to be the one who was troubled by it?

'Are you back in England permanently now?' she
asked.

He shook his head. 'No. Only to keep one or two appointments. I have to see my solicitor.'

He paused, but Frankie was very careful not to
question, or even comment on this. Something to do
with the rights of access to his children, a matter on which
he was so touchy that it was injudicious to press him.
Indeed, she saw, even now, a faint frown appear on his
brow, and the amazing clarity of his eyes cloud for just
a moment. Then he straightened visibly, and the doubts
and shadows were banished, concealed behind a brisk,
authoritative manner.

'I also have to have a check-up with my medical
specialist, which I sincerely hope will be the last,' he
continued with wry self-disgust. Seeing Frankie's eyebrows rise fractionally in a query she wasn't sure it was
even wise to put, he laughed shortly and said, 'According to him, I was suffering from something called
post-traumatic stress syndrome, which the medical profession is only just beginning to recognise and understand. It afflicts such people as soldiers after battle,
survivors of air crashes, or anyone who has been in a
life-threatening situation. Et cetera et cetera.' His tone
was faintly bored, half apologetic, and Frankie was not
taken in by it. He saw this condition as a weakness, and
resented it accordingly. 'You would think I'd be immune
after half a lifetime spent in rough places.'

'Perhaps you were never so critically injured before,'
she suggested cautiously. And he had presumably never

before come home to find out that his wife was being unfaithful to him, as she carefully avoided pointing out.

'That's true,' he said, regarding her thoughtfully. 'Anyhow, I was a very uncooperative and bolshie sort of patient. The doctor has earned his fee.'

'That I can well imagine,' Frankie said with a grin, and was rewarded by an answering smile of blinding relief.

'That's much better! Don't *you* start pussyfooting round me, Frankie, or I shan't know where I'm coming from,' he insisted, and suddenly both of them were laughing.

He was much better, she saw, stronger, more composed, and although the shadows were still there, he knew them for what they were, and was capable of dealing with them. She was astonished anew by how glad this made her, since officially, his personal welfare had little to do with her.

He stood up. 'I must go. I would rather face a trek across the tundra than be stuck in city traffic, but I don't have the luxury of choice.' He paused as she got to her feet, but remained behind her desk, oddly afraid to come out and risk approaching him more closely, for all that part of her longed to do so.

'I'd ask you to have lunch with me, but I already have an appointment,' he said.

'Well . . . another time, perhaps,' Frankie said, careful not to betray too much in the way of disappointment.

The abrupt, decisive, supremely authoritative Julian Tarrant actually hesitated, as if, for once, he had some doubt about the outcome of a directive he was about to make. Then he said, 'What about dinner?'

Frankie was so amazed that her hesitation echoed his, and briefly they looked at one another across a divide which separated not only the one from the other, but both of them from a new and more hopeful relationship.

'Dinner would be lovely, and I happen to be free,' she said graciously, and then, not knowing what mad impulse had seized her, but responding to it instinctively, she said, 'Why don't you be my guest, for a change? I live in Clapham, so I'm not too far out to find.'

'I should be delighted, Frankie,' he said gravely, and with unmistakable sincerity.

Not until after he had left, taking her address with him, scribbled on a scrap of paper, did she sit down, legs collapsing under her, and ask herself, What have I done? She had invited Julian Tarrant into her home, where she lived . . . her sanctuary and refuge, where she escaped from the rigours of the working day!

It wasn't that she had never invited an author home before. But those who had been her guests were the select few whom she knew well enough to count as personal friends—the rest she properly took out to restaurants. Julian Tarrant could not be included among those with whom she felt at ease. He was something else—a man who attracted her, who stirred in her a deep inexplicable awakening of desire.

Frankie took a deep breath and a firm grip on herself. It was useless worrying about intangibles—she had better see to organising the practical side of things.

'Sally!' she called. 'Can you come in? And close the door behind you.'

'Is there a problem?' Sally asked, noting at once the heightened colour and febrile manner that Frankie was unable to hide.

'In a sense.' Frankie paused, but she had to enlist help here. 'I've just done something completely mad. I've invited Julian Tarrant to dinner.'

Her assistant laughed appreciatively. 'That's not mad at all. Having seen him, I don't blame you!'

'Oh, be serious,' Frankie begged. 'I've virtually nothing in the house with which to throw a halfway decent dinner, and there are meetings I can't get out of scheduled all the way through the afternoon, as you very well know. How am I going to shop?'

'You are going to sit down with me and compose a menu, and then I am going to do a dash round Harrods,' Sally said calmly, a gleam in her eyes. She was a gourmet cook who liked nothing better. 'Then I shall shoot over to your place and get the preparations under way.'

'I hoped you would say that,' Frankie said with a sigh of heartfelt relief.

'Think nothing of it. It will be more fun than sitting here typing up readers' reports all afternoon,' Sally chuckled.

As it happened, one of Frankie's meetings ran late, and by the time she got home, for all Sally had done much of the donkey work, it was clear they would have to move quickly to be ready for Julian's seven-thirty arrival. They chopped, peeled, sliced and whipped in virtual silence, and Sally scarcely had time to exercise her perfectly natural curiosity, for which Frankie was grateful.

'Nearly there,' Sally said at last, with satisfaction. 'I'll do the table—you go up and shower and change.'

'Sure?'

'Of course. You can't greet a guest like that, in your office clothes teamed with scruffy slippers and an apron!' Sally grinned. 'Go on—don't waste time.'

Upstairs, Frankie stripped off and showered quickly. Then, still glowing from the hot water, she slipped into flimsy underwear which was all she dared wear under a gold Lycra dress that fitted—but *fitted* everywhere, and took a critical look at herself in her full-length mirror.

Lycra must be the stuff of miracles, she decided. It clung perfectly but never bulged. Or perhaps she really had kept intact the slim figure of her youth, with all the curves in the requisite places. Her stomach was flat, her hips nicely rounded, her breasts firm, and her legs...well, the Lycra had nothing to do with them, as the dress just skimmed her knees, and her Christian Dior gossamer-thin tights emphasised their line and length.

Frankie peered more closely at her face. She was thirty now, and was that a wrinkle she saw when she narrowed her eyes? Certainly not, she thought defiantly. The recent good weather had given her skin a golden sheen so that she required only a slick of moisturiser on her face. Her hair, freshly washed, was silky and highlighted by no other artifice than the sun itself. She applied lipstick and, after a second's hesitation, a spray of the perfume Julian had complained about in France, which she always wore. Accept me as I am, she said inwardly.

A quick glance in the dining-room confirmed that everything was ready. Best crystal glasses and china, candles, a beautiful arrangement of spring flowers.

'Ice in bucket.' Sally ran through the checklist, fastening her jacket at the same time. 'Main course in hostess trolley. Starters and pudding in fridge. Wine ready.'

'You've done wonders,' Frankie said appreciatively.

'Yes, and since I'm not going to be the beneficiary of all this grand organisation, I shall expect a full report on the evening tomorrow morning,' Sally said cheekily. 'I'd better make myself scarce now, before the man arrives. We want him to think you've conjured all this up yourself in the short time since you got home from the office!'

She had not been gone five minutes when the doorbell rang imperatively. Frankie was still scooting round the lounge, making sure it was tidy, and for a few moments she stood rooted stupidly to the spot. It rang again, and at last, feeling as nervous as a fourth-former on her first date, she went to the door.

Julian stood on the doorstep. He had changed from his formal suit into a pair of smart but casual trousers and a jacket. The last of the evening sun gilded his hair, and his blue shirt emphasized the astounding colour of his eyes. He carried a bouquet of early roses which must have cost the earth, expensively packaged in a much-beribbonned cellophane box.

'Aren't you going to ask me in?' he said. 'A man always feels self-conscious enough, carrying these things through the streets!'

'Of course.' She stood aside, closed the door behind him, and then he followed her through into the lounge. 'I do appreciate your suffering—they're lovely.'

She went through the motions of putting the flowers in water and fixing gin and tonics for both of them. It was impossible for her not to be intensely aware of him all the while, sitting there, long legs stretched out, one hand resting on the arm of his chair. She saw him taking in the gold Lycra dress, the way it clung and flattered and was enhanced by her slight tan and the silken sheen of her hair. She could feel him mentally adjusting his image of her. He had never seen her this way before. Wasn't that what you intended, she asked herself nervously, to correct the picture?

'You have a very pleasant home here, Frankie?' he said. 'Have you lived here for long?'

'Several years. I like it, but compared to Cerne Farm it's nothing grand. I don't seem to have an awful lot of time to devote to working out artistic colour schemes and the like.'

'That's not important—I think it's comfortable and delightful,' he said. 'With the hours you must put in for Cooper Masterman, obviously you don't have time to stitch matching cushion covers! You mustn't put yourself down, Frankie.'

It was on the tip of Frankie's tongue to say, I don't usually need to, when you're around. She bit firmly on the comment, determined, for this one evening, to have an embargo on recriminations, snide remarks or anything else which might poison the atmosphere. But she was beginning to think she had gone over the top with the dress. Sitting there with him, showing a fair amount of leg and cleavage, every bit as though she had dressed up for an intimate evening *à deux* instead of entertaining an author. Maybe she should have worn something less revealing, more conservative?

She smiled and deliberately shook off her misgivings. She was not a teenager. Being alone with a man had held no terrors for her previously, and should hold none now. She hoped her voice was steady as she said, 'You're right, of course. Shall we go through into the dining-room?'

Carefully, making sure to keep her hand steady, Frankie served the chilled crab, tomato and avocado soup, together with a half-bottle of a newly available spicy white Moravian wine.

'This is very unusual,' he said, sipping appreciatively.

'Sally introduced me to it. She's a connoisseuse of viniculture, among other things. In fact, to be honest, I couldn't have had this meal on the table in time without her help.'

'How very refreshing,' he said.

'Isn't it?'

'No—I meant you, not the wine,' he said seriously. 'A lot of women would have gone to great lengths to claim the credit all for themselves. But you are ... disconcertingly honest. And fair.'

Now she knew she was blushing, confound it, and hoped the soft glow of the candlelight would hide some of her confusion from him.

'That would be silly. I don't stand or fall, in my own estimation, on my cuisine,' she said. 'I can cook well enough, as it happens, but my self-esteem doesn't depend on it.'

'What does it depend on, then?' he asked unexpectedly. Frankie, taking the lamb noisettes from the heated trolley and pouring a Spanish Navarra forceful enough not to be defeated by the combination of mild spices in the sauce, was arrested by the sudden intimation that this line of questioning was not just dinner-table talk. That he really did want to know.

'Being respected in my profession, for one thing,' she answered carefully. 'Having good friends, and being one. Trying to be a happy and worthwhile human being, I suppose—if that doesn't sound too pretentious.' She slid back into her chair, to find his eyes still fixed contemplatively on her.

Beginning to feel a little disconcerted by this subject, she said briskly, 'Enough about me. I am really a very straightforward, uncomplicated person. What you see is what you get.' She smiled. 'How about you? Tell me—how did it go with the specialist?'

He shrugged. 'Physically, I'm fit for a normal existence, but I knew that anyhow. Cold, damp weather might give me the odd twinge, but I can deal with that. There's a steel plate somewhere in my left leg, and I'm pinned and reconstructed so that here and there I resemble the Bionic Man, so I must measure the amount of exertion to which I subject the technology.' He laughed—it was a little hollow, but not so bitter as Frankie remembered. 'It isn't as bad as it sounds. I could probably play cricket, but not rugby, I can ride, although not in the Grand National. And from now on I travel first class.'

The gently ironic humour in his tone prompted Frankie to risk asking, 'And what about the . . . what did you call it . . . post . . . ?'

'Post-traumatic stress. I appear to be over it.' She saw, or perhaps only imagined that she saw him flinch slightly. 'I no longer wake in the night sweating and shaking and reliving unpleasant experiences. In short, I can get on with my life.'

'That's wonderful news,' she said warmly.

'I'm not so sure. It means I no longer have an official excuse for being morose or bad-tempered, or just plain beastly to everyone.' His tone was still mildly jocular, but there was a serious note underlying it. 'I can no longer expect people to say, well, poor old Julian, he's had a bad time and he's not too well. Go easy on him.'

He was poking fun at himself, and at the same time taking himself to task with such perceptive accuracy that she caught her breath. Not until later, when they had disposed of the marsala-drowned syllabub and moved back to the lounge for coffee, did she find the courage to say, 'Since you are now this reformed paragon of mild-mannered amiability, is it in order for me to ask if your meeting with the solicitor was equally successful?'

For a moment she thought she had pushed her luck too far. The powerful frame tensed slightly, then mercifully relaxed, and he said, 'Up to a point. My son and daughter are allowed to spend some time with me at Cerne Farm, this summer. It's a beginning, I suppose.'

He leaned forward. 'Have you ever been married, Frankie?'

She laughed. 'Very briefly, when I was a student. We were far too young, it was a silly idea, and we cut our losses before we were in too deep.'

'So you didn't have children?'

'No.' Her brow furrowed briefly. 'I wanted a baby, although that too would not have been very sensible, since we were both strapped financially and still studying for our finals. But the moment I mentioned it, Tom made it clear he wanted out. Oh, I don't resent him for it. The whole thing was a mistake. Anyhow, he went to Canada on a research fellowship, stayed there and eventually re-married. I still get a card on my birthday and at Christmas, and I have a standing invitation to visit if I'm ever over there.'

'And would you?'

'Why not?' She shrugged. 'There are no residual feelings, hard or otherwise. It's just something that happened a long time ago. I wish him all the best—I imagine he feels the same about me.'

'How marvellously civilised!' He stood up, obviously still needing some form of release from tension, and rested one elbow on the mantel, looking down at her. 'I suppose divorce need not be acrimonious when there are no children involved, and no third party. Let's just say my experience was different.'

Frankie shifted slightly on the edge of the sofa. He was once again too close, too male, and she felt the physical spell of him enmeshing her ever more closely.

'Didn't you . . . didn't you sort out things like access rights and so on at the time of the divorce? From what one hears, I believe it's usual to do so,' she said practically, fighting hard to keep a grip on her wayward senses.

'Maybe it is, but I wasn't in any state to think clearly at the time,' he said shortly. 'I just wanted the quickest way out of a marriage which had gone sour on me.'

His fingers tapped the mantelshelf, and she saw him wrestling with two needs—one, to remain withdrawn, private and inviolate, and another, quite contrary, to confide and perhaps exorcise.

'I married the girl next door—well, at least, the girl from the house over the hill,' he said. 'We were childhood sweethearts, and I suppose everyone took it for granted we would marry. Aside from the odd youthful adventure, when boys would be boys, I never bothered with another woman. I believed, quite seriously, that Alison and I were for life, whatever happened. Coming back from Amazonia to learn that she had someone else was, quite simply, shattering.'

'Caesar's wife,' she said softly, her mind casting back to that warm evening in the Languedoc. When his eyebrows rose in question, she said, 'She had to be beyond reproach. You couldn't have...forgiven her?'

'It never crossed my mind,' he said in some surprise, as if the idea were revolutionary.

No, it would not have—not with this hard, straight, uncompromising man. For him, things had to be perfect, or not at all. Perhaps Alison Tarrant had found him too much to live up to? But having known him all her life, shouldn't she have expected that?

'Have some more coffee,' she said shakily.

'No...thank you.' He sat down unexpectedly next to her, and she was overcome by a weakness that was frightening and pleasurable at the same time. The last time they had been this close, he had kissed her savagely, and she knew beyond question that he was thinking of it, too. Remembering the feel of her, as she was remembering him.

He said slowly, 'I have to explain something to you, Frankie...something that is difficult for me, but has to be said. Having by necessity to accept a complete change of lifestyle...and then, Alison...well, you know, it was as if the two things that had most defined me as a man had been taken from me, at a stroke. It's what we were saying at dinner...my self-esteem, my image of my own worth, had gone. What was I? That was how I felt when you visited me at Cerne Farm, and how I felt when you saw me in France. Am I making sense?'

She swallowed hard.

'Yes and no. I realised you were bitter. I never felt that you were in any way...emasculated.'

On the contrary. The prickling of her skin the first time his fingers ever touched hers, those moments in the storm-ravaged house, crackling with sensuality, when for two pins she would have been in his arms. His fierce, punishing kisses in the study...oh, no, you were never less than a man, she thought. You were more man than I could handle, and you still are...

He reached out one hand and laid it on her shoulder, sliding it across the bare skin of her neck to cup the nape, his fingers pushing up into the thick locks of hair that curled around it.

'I can tell you, I certainly don't feel that way right now...Francesca,' he said.

She shivered, and laughed shakily.

'Oh, please don't call me that! I abandoned it long ago, because it doesn't suit me. I ought to have long black hair and smouldering Latin eyes, with a name like that...' she prattled on inanely, trying to ignore the thumping of her heart. 'I ought to look like an Italian...'

'Shut up,' said Julian Tarrant firmly but amiably, and he then ensured her complete obedience to this command by covering her mouth with his. Not roughly this time, he did not hurt her, but with utter authority he went on kissing her until she was breathless, her lips parting under the persuasive pressure of his.

Frankie was helpless with delight. This was not fantasy, not longing; this was real. At last, she had what she could not deny she had craved for since the day they met—his arms around her, his warm, strong body strained to hers, the blissful feel of his muscles beneath her hands as her arms snaked around his back.

They leaned back together, moving as one; she was stretched out beneath him, welcoming the heaviness of him, wanting more and more of it. She arched her neck as he covered her throat with kisses, and moaned with unseemly eagerness as his hands worked the dress down over her shoulders. Taut with desire as he unclipped the minimal bra, her breasts aching for his touch, she cried out softly as he possessed them with his hands. Reaching up, she clasped her own hands at the back of his neck, as his mouth found its way to her breast. There had never been sensation to compare with how she felt right now, she had never before been so supremely a woman as she was at this moment, desperate to be taken, to be his, and to stake her own answering claim on him.

He lifted his head and looked down into her eyes. His own were narrowed and dark with intent passion, a purposeful insistence which sent a wild thrill coursing through her.

'I can't make love to you here, Frankie,' he said in a voice harsh with need. 'It isn't comfortable...there isn't enough room. The bedroom...'

If he had simply gone ahead and taken her, there and then, letting the momentum carry them forward, regardless of the physical limitations of a two-seater couch for a six-foot-four man, all would have been well. As it was, the sudden and unexpected halt broke the spell, and Frankie was all at once aghast at what she was doing.

She was in the lounge in her own living-room, behaving with an abandon that was almost indecent. One moment they had been having coffee, the next she was half naked. One moment they had not been quite friends, the next they were very nearly lovers. If she had ever imagined taking a lover in this house, she had hazily envisaged that there would be a measure of commitment...it would not be a one-night stand, or a crazy surrender to a physical need so urgent she could barely see straight for it...

'Julian, listen, no...we can't...not like this!' she protested insistently, pressing both hands against his chest.

'That's exactly what I'm saying, Frankie!' he laughed, biting her earlobe. 'So let's go upstairs, right now. God, don't make me wait much longer—I can't stand it! I've got to have you! It's driving me mad!'

Frankie's own desire had built up into a pitch where she had been just about ready to explode into a thousand pieces. It would have been the easiest thing in the world just to surrender to what she so urgently wanted, and she almost wished he would take her by force, so she would need to do nothing but give in. But her mind was working now, and it was telling her that she should *not* just give in, that it was all too much, too soon, and that she would only regret her too ready capitulation.

'I can't!' she gasped agonisedly. 'We really hardly know each other...and until tonight weren't even sure we liked each other! It's all happening too quickly!' She looked up at him, real panic in her eyes. 'I know you have this notion that I'm streetwise and sophisticated, but there hasn't been anyone in ages, and I'm scared...'

The sofa creaked as he sat up, releasing her from his weight.

'You're serious, aren't you?' he said half disgustedly. As she nodded in mute despair, he went on, low-voiced, 'We're adult people, Frankie. You invited me here, laid on a superb meal, with you in a dress seductive enough to lead a saint astray. And then you allowed me to go so far without discouraging me...on the contrary. Now you're behaving all of a sudden like a nervous virgin, trying to make out it's never happened to you before.'

This faintly offensive insinuation brought Frankie angrily to her senses, and she snapped, 'You can believe what you damn well like, but I don't bring men here and let them take me to bed at the drop of a hat!'

His eyes raked over her, cool, now, but knowing, reminding her of her dishevelment, of her half-naked body still exposed to his gaze.

'In that case, hadn't you better put your clothes on?' he said, on a note of weary indifference, and standing up, he made a point of turning away while she scrambled inelegantly back into her bra, and pulled her dress back on to her shoulders.

She had never felt so despairing, so shamed, and, what was worse, so strung out with unsatisfied need as she did now, gazing at his stubbornly turned back. It was useless to deny that she had been attracted to him from the day they met, with little hope, for most of that time, that he would ever seriously feel the same about her. And now, tonight, they had seemed to draw closer to one another, he had confided in her as never before...and they had ignited a fierce spark of mutual desire. And she, with her own nervous ineptitude, had blown it out.

'Julian,' she said quietly, unable to keep the note of pleading from her voice, 'let's not be angry with each other. It wasn't a rejection. I did...do...feel very strongly attracted to you. How could you fail to know it? It's just that...I need time. There are some things it doesn't seem right just to go ahead and do, regardless.'

He turned, shrugged, and slung her admission coldly back in her face.

'That's nonsense. There are times when the only way is dead ahead...or dead stop,' he contradicted bluntly. 'But I'm not angry, Frankie, I assure you. I don't suppose I'm the first man in history to have miscalculated my chances, and I won't be the last. As rejections go, I've known far worse. Don't lose any sleep over it— I shan't.'

No, I'll bet you won't, she thought, boiling up again with furious humiliation. It had not meant all that much to him, truly. They had been alone, after an intimate dinner with plenty of wine, he had felt better, fit and in command of himself again, and ready to prove to himself that he was once more a man, in every sense. She supposed he had found her attractive enough for the purpose. She would do as well as anyone.

'If that's the importance women have in your scheme of things, you shouldn't have been too surprised your wife found someone else,' she said acidly.

She had done it again, and she knew at once that it was a taunt unworthy of her, but she was hurting herself, shamed by his casual manner and compelled by a need to hit back. But he floored her completely, with a lift of the eyebrows and a faint, off-hand smile.

'What a close-knit freemasonry you women share,' he observed disparagingly. 'That's more or less what *she* said to me, over lunch. I thought perhaps *you* were different. But when it comes down to fundamentals, you're all tarred with the same brush. Small-minded, self-centred, and not really worth the effort of taking seriously!'

CHAPTER SEVEN

AFTER he had gone, Frankie mechanically cleared away the remains of the dinner, stacked and programmed the dishwasher, hung up her dress, pulled on her dressing-gown, and made herself a cup of decaffeinated coffee which she hoped would be soporific. She did not think it would be very effective.

'I have a lunch appointment,' he had told her that morning in her office, and oh, yes, he had! With his ex-wife, no less! I was no more than a diversion, Frankie told herself crossly. He was still hung-up on Alison, and no doubt he had realised that when he met her again. So he had decided to try a little therapy to take his mind off this continuing obsession...he thought he would boost his ego by trying his luck with another woman. And that was where *she* had come into the picture!

She realised that she was biting her lip and gripping her mug furiously, and with a surprised little shake of the head she thought, this one was not for fun...she really did care.

'No!' she protested fiercely, aloud, then she sighed, her shoulders sagged, and, 'Yes,' she admitted, in a quieter voice. But it was totally pointless. She might as well forget it. Hitching up her dressing-gown to prevent herself from tripping over the hem, she turned disconsolately towards the stairs.

Huddled in a corner of her bed, hands clasped tightly around her knees, Frankie stared unseeing at the patterns of light the street-lamp outside cast on the ceiling.

'Heaven help me, I think I love him,' she confessed silently. How had it come to this? She had been seriously in love only once, with Tom, when she was eighteen, but then everyone fell in love at eighteen, it was practically obligatory, and almost everyone recovered. It wasn't terminal. At eighteen, one's resilient young heart bounced back and came up fighting. Frankie's had, even though she had been wiser and chastened, and with a broken marriage to show for the experience.

Since then, she had avoided the condition, and to be honest it had not been all that difficult to do so. She had been busy and involved, climbing the ladder of her career, and no one had got close enough to touch her heart, or inflame her senses beyond a manageable point.

But this—the love that hit you in your mature years— this was different. You couldn't roll with the punches and tell yourself, so what, he doesn't care, someone else will be along. The heart grew more selective with time, it gave itself only where it was really sure, even though it knew there was no help for it. This wound would never truly heal, although it might outwardly appear to, or she might pretend that it had. It would rupture and break open, again and again.

'Damnation!' Frankie slid down into the bed, pulling the duvet up to her ears, hugging herself tight against the pain of this unwanted realisation. He had attracted her, against all common sense, within minutes of their meeting, and she had actively desired him ever since. Well, tonight she could have satisfied that desire. She could have let him make love to her, and her body still ached with the memory of his touch, the pleasure that had almost taken her over the edge.

But what would that have solved? He might or he might not still have wanted her afterwards. It might not have been just a one-night fling. But for all she could perhaps have engaged his desire for a while, she did not believe she could have torn his inner passion from the woman who still ruled it, despite all she had done to him.

Alison, damn her, who had had his love all her life, who had borne his children, who had betrayed and nearly destroyed him, and who, even now, he could not completely let go.

I don't want to simply sleep with him a few times and have what the world calls an affair, Frankie moaned to herself in the darkness. I want to be with him every night, to be filled with him, to be the one he turns to if the shadows ever recur. To help him rebuild a life, to argue and fight and disagree and laugh, to surrender the inviolate core of myself, which no one has ever been able to wrest from me. I want to love him—but he would never, ever permit me to, never mind love me in return.

The answer was... that there was no answer, Frankie told herself next morning, peering bleary eyed into the bathroom mirror after a restless, tossing night. The previous day's sunny weather had turned coat and become a damp, soggy apology for spring, and how was it that her tan, which yesterday had been golden, was beginning to look sallow? Grudgingly she slapped on make-up, dragged a brush through her tousled locks and climbed woodenly into her career-woman's uniform before hurriedly drinking a cup of tea, standing up at the breakfast bar in the kitchen. No doubt the trains would all be full of disgruntled commuters—and she felt about a hundred and two as it was! She looked at her watch, and remembered that she had a production meeting at the printers for which she was sure to be late. It was going to be that kind of a day!

One meeting led to another, and at lunchtime Frankie finally made the office, grabbing a sandwich and a cup of coffee to have at her desk while she caught up with her piling up paperwork. She had to face the brightly curious Sally, too, who was about to go out on her lunch break, but who had obviously hung on to hear about the dinner.

'Well?'

'Well, what?'

'Oh, come on!' Sally was not to be fobbed off that easily. 'How did it go?'

Frankie sighed. Having enlisted and been grateful for Sally's help, she could not now expect to go all tight-lipped on her.

'The dinner was brilliant—thanks to you, in no small measure,' she said. 'As a social occasion, all I can say is that it was a bit fraught. I must have been a fool to think I could ever get along with that man.'

Sally glanced quickly into the outer office, before closing the door.

'That nosy Morag is hanging about out there,' she said. 'She's the office gossip; you don't want her listening in to anything you wouldn't want to broadcast on the *News at Ten*! But do tell—what happened?'

'Not a lot,' Frankie lied. Sally was a friend and confidante, up to a point, as well as her assistant, but she could not have endured rehashing for anyone else's ears her abortive seduction scene with Julian! 'Julian Tarrant and I are simply chalk and cheese—but then, I knew that all along.'

'I think there's more to it than that, but if you don't want to tell me I can't force you to,' Sally said philosophically.

Alone again, Frankie sighed once more and returned to her paperwork. The offices were quiet, most people being out at lunch, and she jumped when the phone shrilled on her desk, having forgotten that she had asked Sally to switch it through to her.

'Frankie?'

She started again at the sound of his voice, so clear that he might have been standing behind her.

'Hello, Julian.' Her reply was calm, but carefully non-committal, assuming nothing and giving nothing away.

He said, 'I don't know if you would expect me to do the gentlemanly thing, but this is as close as I can get. I can't and don't apologise for anything I did . . . or tried to do last night, but if you found my attitude unpleasant, put it down to thwarted male pride.'

She tried to inject a casual nonchalance into her reply, to make out that it was no big deal.

'Forget it. It was just one of those things,' she said briskly. 'It was my responsibility as much as yours, anyhow. I hope it need not interfere with our working relationship in any way.'

'There's no reason why it should, especially as I'm off back to France first thing tomorrow. I'll be in touch when necessary. Thank you for the first-rate dinner. We can write off the rest to experience.'

She put down the phone a little sadly. She had been happier with the caustic rancour with which they had parted last night—at least that had indicated some feeling. But this polite detachment, implying that a moment's lust had led them temporarily to make fools of themselves, only emphasised how little the whole thing had meant to him.

Put it down to thwarted male pride ... forget it ... just one of those things. But I love him, she thought bewilderedly. Already she was smarting from the pain of separation, from knowing that she would not be seeing him again in who knew how long. And beneath that raw agony lay the deeper anguish of knowing that he was not in any way hers, and never would be. Oh, hell! Frankie thumped her fist down on the desk and bit back tears she had never thought a thirty-year-old woman would feel the need to cry. Why did life have to be so full of problems? Why did she have to love a man who was flying off to Toulouse in the morning without a second thought for her?

A day or so later, when she happened to be conferring with Ivor in his office, he suddenly looked sharply at her through the glitter of his spectacles, and said, 'Incidentally, I wonder if you are aware that there is a rumour going the rounds about you?'

He spoke lightly, but nothing Ivor said was ever truly light or intended to be taken that way, so Frankie paid full attention to the warning signals her own brain was sending her.

'Oh, really?' she said. 'What am I supposed to have done? Been put forward for the Nobel prize in literature? Got caught red-handed watching blue movies in the video library?'

Ivor's thin lips moved in their habitual apology for a smile.

'Word has it that you and Julian Tarrant are conducting a torrid affair,' he said, the very dryness of his voice reducing the idea to something sordid.

Frankie laughed shortly, her mind racing as she tried to work out how such a story had got started.

'It never ceases to amaze me what mean little minds there are engaged in what is supposed to be an adult business,' she replied, her voice cool, concealing a furious mortification. 'It really is pathetic that their owners have nothing better to do than to circulate silly tittle-tattle.'

Ivor paid little attention to this cold blast of condemnation.

'Of course,' he went on regardless, as if she had not spoken, 'we are not doctors or lawyers. There is no breach of professional ethics, as such, and what my staff do in their own time is their own business. Nevertheless——'

'Ivor,' Frankie said heavily, 'are you listening to me? I am not—repeat, *not*—having an affair with Julian Tarrant.'

'I merely asked if you were aware of the gossip,' he said cleverly. 'I did not say I subscribed to it. It isn't necessary to over-react.'

'Over-react?' Frankie kept her voice low and her indignation on a tight rein, but inwardly, she was quivering with outrage. 'If this ridiculous story gains any more ground, and I catch whoever is responsible for spreading it, I won't over-react, I'll sue! If something like this gets around, it will do my professional reputation no good at all. Half my male authorship won't feel safe with me, and the other half will think I'm a pushover!'

Ivor looked measuringly at her, saw she was deadly serious, and showed his mettle.

'All right, Frankie, I'll squash it firmly, in so far as I can,' he said. 'You are a good editor, and you deserve to get on, unhindered by this sort of pettiness.'

Mollified only in part, Frankie strode briskly back to her office, called Sally in, and asked her to close the door.

'It's obvious from your expression that you've heard this silly rumour that's going around,' she said wryly. 'For heaven's sake, Sally, why didn't you tell me?'

'You looked as if you were already carrying half the cares of the world on your shoulders,' Sally said wretchedly. 'I didn't want to worry you any further. It must have been Morag—she was listening outside the door the other day, and she's always ready to add up two and two to make five.' She cast Frankie a shrewd glance. 'These things usually die of their own accord, given a day or so,' she said. 'I don't know why you're so uptight—unless, of course, there's a grain of truth in it.'

'Sally,' Frankie said heavily, 'watch my lips. I am *not* having an affair with Julian. Even if I were contemplating it, it would be a complete waste of time, since he's still having one with his ex-wife, in every way that counts! Furthermore, you can let it be known out there, in the gossip factory, that I shall personally jump on anyone I catch spreading malicious nonsense about me!'

She left it at that, hoping that the word would go back along the grapevine in the opposite direction. If a few speculative glances were cast her way by people as they passed her along the corridors, she ignored them.

In part, she felt something of a hypocrite, for very easily, she knew, she might have been having an affair with Julian Tarrant, and at least half of her wished it were true. But it wasn't, and she did not see why she should have the name without the game.

The summer advanced, days brightening and lengthening, and developing, in July, into a full-blown heatwave, when all London worked with its shirt-sleeves rolled up and its windows wide open, and the same people who had grumbled about the rain and the cold grew bad-tempered and crochety on account of the heat. There was no respite from the blazing pavements, and frozen food defrosted drippingly on its way home from the supermarket. In the still stuffy evenings, Frankie sat out in her garden and fantasised about fresh green countryside and cool lakes, but she had far too much work on hand to hope to get away anywhere before the autumn.

And in all this time, she heard nothing at all from Julian. Not a word. She told herself there was no reason why he should contact her. He had said the manuscript would be in by September, and if he had no problems he did not need to communicate with her.

Against all hope, she had hoped for a personal line or two—anything. That she was disappointed only proved that he did not think about her in that way, despite the undeniable physical attraction which had flared between them on several occasions. Despite the evening at her house, when they had almost made love. He had obviously written that off as an unfortunate error of judgement, and forgotten about it. All he had been trying to do, after all, was to take his mind off his meeting with Alison.

Oh, but... he had seemed so relaxed, that evening. He had emanated the renewed confidence of a man who had his life back on the rails. He had even talked about his ex-wife, and about the effect her desertion had had on him, with relative objectivity. And all the time, the truth was that seeing her again had fired him with a need to prove his manhood. He had come to Frankie with the express intention of using *her* for that purpose.

No! She couldn't bear to think that way about those few moments of what had seemed to her to be a spontaneous explosion of passion and mutual need. Maybe it would be better for her if she could see it reduced to its lowest common denominator, but she was stubbornly and stupidly reluctant to part with the little she had of him—the memories. And so she suffered and went on living, which was all she could sensibly do.

Somehow, she dragged herself through the hot days in her hot office and the stifling nights that robbed her of the only peace she could hope to find—the oblivion of sleep. And then, one day, a bombshell landed on her doormat in the form of a large padded envelope, the kind authors used to post their manuscripts.

Frankie picked it up and turned it over in her hands. It was postmarked Bournemouth-Poole, and her heart jerked with excitement, because she had already recognised the bold, forthright handwriting on the address. Julian was back in England.

Had he finished his book earlier than expected? But if so, why would he send it here, to her home address, rather than to the offices of Cooper Masterman? Frankie opened it with eager care, and saw, to her utter amazement, that what she held in her trembling hands was Julian Tarrant's journal.

Enclosed was a note.

'I'd like you to read this,' he wrote, no 'dear Frankie', no preamble, straight down to it—'and give me your opinion. I know I said I would never publish, but I've come to the conclusion that perhaps I should—that my life is bound up with the book I'm writing, and that this personal trivia is part and parcel of it. Omitting it has come to seem dishonest.

'All I have held back is what I wrote about my marriage and its breakdown. I felt it would be no act of a gentleman to lay that open to the world.

'I'm sorry this is handwritten, but I don't type, and I did not want anyone else to read it before you did. I shall be here at Cerne Farm. Phone me.'

To the point, with every request framed more in the nature of a command. And even now still respecting the sensibilities of the woman who had not given a damn for his. Frankie smiled, shaken by her own tender feelings. He would never change, nor, now, would she essentially want him to.

She sat in the garden in the warm after-dinner twilight, with moths fluttering like wraiths around the patio lamps, and read until the moon was high in a dark sky. Then she made herself cocoa and went upstairs, where she continued reading in bed until the birds began carolling an early dawn. How she was going to get through the day after such a night, she did not know, but she had been compelled to reach the end, and this need only confirmed what her snatched glimpses back in the cottage in France had promised her. She read on until the final drama, deep in the Amazonian jungles.

Julian Tarrant did not spare himself. Forward planning had given his expedition no hint of guerrilla activity near the area they had planned to penetrate, but, notwithstanding that, he blamed himself for leading his party into the thick of a dispute between rival groups who had so terrorised the local Indian tribes that they had been forced to flee their ancestral lands. He, Julian, should have known, somehow, what even government agencies did not—by clairvoyance, perhaps? Frankie wondered ruefully.

Having discovered the danger, he should have withdrawn at once, but he was so incensed by the Indians' plight that he wanted to contact them and learn more about it, in order to help. This he never achieved, for one terrible day his party found themselves in the middle of a grim shoot-out between the two guerrilla bands, and as the battle progressed it became frighteningly obvious that they would simply be mown down by automatic gunfire if they could not escape.

What happened next, he told simply and without heroics. It was stupid—the action of a fool, and he was fortunate not to have been killed outright, leaving his party in a worse plight than ever. He tied a white shirt to a pole—cliché tactics, as he drily described it—and, hoisting it aloft, walked out into the midst of the action to negotiate a ceasefire long enough for him and his associates to get clear of the area. Inevitably, he stopped a stray bullet in the thigh. Inevitably, it got no more than rudimentary treatment when he was taken captive by the closest of the guerrilla groups.

'If the shooting seems to have stopped for any appreciable time, get out of here, fast,' he had told his second-in-command firmly, 'and that's an order. I'll

catch up with you. They have to let me go. I'm of no
conceivable use to them.'

The hiatus caused by the sheer effrontery of this
strange intruder was brief, but the members of the expedition did as they were told, and made their escape—
on a trek, Julian Tarrant was supreme commander, a
dictator, not a democrat. But he found himself blind-
folded, tied to a tree, and to all intents and purposes
condemned to imminent execution. He felt the cold steel
of a pistol against his temple, and the world went black—
from loss of blood, from fear, or from a potent combination of the two—he could not have said which.

For whatever reason, they spared him, he never knew
why. When he regained consciousness, he was alone and
the fighting had moved on. He could hear it raging in
the distance, and knew he had to work fast to free himself
and escape, in case they came back and decided it would
be as well to finish himself off.

Julian knew enough basic first-aid to strap himself up
so that he was mobile—just. The account of his lone
trek back through the vast forests, slowed by his injury,
in severe pain, and at the end almost delirious, made
gruesome and gripping reading.

The fact that he made it back at all, he in no way
considered a triumph. To him, his entire part in the affair
was a failure. It was not his business to go stumbling
around in the jungle getting wounded and imperilling
the lives of others. His business was to learn, report,
and add to the sum total of knowledge about the natural
world.

Nor did he gloss over the mental trauma which had
bedevilled him only after he was safe home, the black
nights when he awoke and relived the whole terrifying

episode again, not in dreams, but *as if it were still happening*. The only thing he had salvaged from it all was a deeper knowledge of himself, of his own resources and limitations, than most people could hope to glean in a lifetime.

It was powerful stuff. Frankie read it through again the following night, just to be sure that her first impressions were true, and in no way swayed by her own emotional involvement. She was quite, quite sure, but by then it was two in the morning, so she set Julian's manuscript on her bedside table, and with a smile on her face, settled down for the best night's sleep she had had in weeks.

She had planned to phone him first thing, but it was Saturday, and sheer exhaustion had made her sleep late. Waiting only long enough to make herself a strong pot of tea, she looked up Julian's Cerne Farm number in her address book and picked up the receiver.

At Cerne Farm, the phone rang and rang. After so long, the pain of almost making contact seared her afresh, and then, just as she was about to give up, he answered.

'Julian... it's Frankie.' She gripped the receiver as if she were holding his hand and wanted never to let go.

'Frankie. Are you well?'

'Fine... I'm... fine.' She gulped. 'Julian, I read your manuscript, and it's... incredible. I can't find words to do it justice.'

'Shortage of words must be a new and serious condition for you, Frankie.' There was humour in his voice, but she thought she discerned a note of pleasure, too. On account solely of her admiration of his work, or was he just a little pleased to hear her voice? Wishful thinking, Frankie, she warned herself.

'It's my opinion that we should not treat this as a separate entity, but try to find a way of bringing it into the existing book,' she said. 'That will give it just the impact needed to set the whole thing ablaze. Shall I write to you about it at greater length when I'm back in the office on Monday?'

'No, don't do that,' he said unexpectedly. 'I'd rather we discussed this properly, in person. Come down next weekend, if you're free.'

The thought of spending the weekend at Cerne Farm, of being once again under the same roof, seeing him, talking to him, filled Frankie with such anxious delight that she feared for herself. All the same, she demurred.

'But didn't you say something about having your children with you?'

'Indeed. They are here,' he affirmed.

'Then you won't want me around...' she hesitated.

'I wish you would come, Frankie,' he said quietly. 'Please. It would take some of the pressure off, to be perfectly honest. Things are a little fraught. I'm not used to being a full-time father. And you and I really do need to talk about this book.'

She would, in any event, have found him difficult to refuse. And since he had actually said 'please' for once in his life, she found it impossible to do anything but agree.

If he were surprised by her swift capitulation, he gave no sign of it.

'How will you come? Will you drive down?' he asked.

'I don't even own a car,' she told him laughingly. 'Living where I do, I don't have much call for one. I could hire one, I suppose. Or if I felt really masochistic, I could brave your rural bus service.'

He actually joined in her laughter.

'Don't worry. Come by train and I'll meet you at the station in Poole,' he offered. 'The train times may well have changed since I was last here. I'll look them up and phone your secretary when I've figured out the best one for you to arrive on.'

'No, don't do that,' she said quickly. She did not doubt Sally's discretion, but the last thing she wanted, the very last, was to start up any more talk at the office by letting it be known that she was spending the weekend at Canford Tarrant. Calls came through the secretarial pool before being put through to individual editors, and Frankie was taking no chances of anyone listening in. Besides, Sally already had her suspicions about her and Julian, and it would be best not to stir them up. 'I'll call you,' she told him, deciding that this was one call she would definitely be making from home. Then, as she sensed him speculating about her reluctance, she said, 'We don't want any guesswork about this around the office until I've discussed it with you and your decision to publish is absolutely definite.'

She walked back into the kitchen in a daze. For her, the morning was golden and unsullied. She was going to see Julian again. It might not be very much... considering how very much she loved and desired him, but it had to be enough, and briefly, she was ecstatic.

On a hot, brilliantly sunny afternoon in early August, the train bringing Frankie from London crossed the narrow spit of land separating Poole from the shimmering blue expanse of its lovely harbour. She looked out over endless green inlets into which the azure fingers stole lazily, the humped, mysterious shape of Brownsea Island in the centre, and across the bay, the silhouetted houses of Sandbanks, looking almost Mediterranean in the heat haze.

Gazing at the myriad bright sails of the yachts out on the water, Frankie, briefly envious, thought that this must be a lovely part of the world to live in, and she understood all too well what had drawn Julian back.

The train slowed as the track negotiated the level crossing that bisected the town's high street, and as it pulled decorously into the station Frankie reached her weekend case down from the luggage rack.

She looked cool and crisp in a narrow, sleeveless black slip of a dress, placket buttons open at the throat to display a slender, three rope gold chain, her feet in open-toed strappy black sandals. Inwardly, she was as excited as a three-year-old going to her first party, and equally as nervous.

It was all so different from the last time she had dismounted here, all those months ago, in the cold, blustery rain, when she had taken the bus through the dismal, sodden countryside.

And yet perhaps not so different, because here he was, the man she had gone so reluctantly to meet on that other occasion, whose presence had drawn her back here once again. Striding down the platform towards her in cotton twill trousers and a short-sleeved shirt, upright and confident, hair gleaming in the sun. Julian Tarrant, the man she was proud to love, although she dared not show it. The man who had turned her life inside out.

If she had wondered, just for one minute during the journey, if things might have changed, if she had hoped that her feelings might not be so intense, since, for her own sake, it would be better if she did not care so much, all such thoughts deserted her now. If anything, it was worse, because the last time they were together she had not realised, or at least had not admitted to herself that she loved him.

Well, she knew now. There was no escaping it or turning away from it, or pretending that it did not exist. He had proved to be all too easy a man to love. All she could do was accept it—and above all, keep it firmly and resolutely to herself.

CHAPTER EIGHT

THE rhododendrons had finished, but the roses were in full bloom in the gardens of Cerne Farm. The lawns had been mown, the shrubs trimmed, and the impression now was of a home where people lived, rather than of an empty house inhabited only by ghosts.

The brilliant sunshine helped, of course. But in the main, it was Julian, his energy-charged personality, his uplifted confidence, that was responsible for the vital difference. Frankie could hardly believe that the morose, embittered individual she had found holed up here last winter, barricaded against the world and his own feelings, and this forceful, quietly humorous man with his blue eyes agleam, were one and the same person.

'I have come to a decision that this place should be farmed properly again,' he told her as they piled out of the estate car. 'For too long it has been Cerne Farm in name only. I was always away too often to keep an eye on it, and Alison was never interested in the possibilities, either.'

'Yes, I can just visualise you striding about in your Barbour and wellies, waxing enthusiastic about crop rotation and milk quotas,' Frankie grinned, and his answering smile set her heart thumping agitatedly, as if her ribcage were too fragile to confine it.

'I never said I was going to do it myself,' he demurred. 'I won't have time or inclination to turn bucolic.

134

I shall put a good manager in and let him get on with it, while I keep a watching brief.'

Before Frankie had the chance to ask him what was going to keep him so busy that he would be short of time, a girl of about thirteen, flaxen-blonde and tall, came round from the back of the house, leading a pony.

'My daughter, Karin,' Julian said. 'I thought I told you, young lady—no horses round the front. They kick up the lawn.'

'Right you are!' she said with mild impudence, and then, looking a little more shyly at Frankie, 'Hi.'

'Hi. I'm Frankie Somers,' Frankie replied. 'Nice to meet you.'

Karin regarded her curiously. 'Do you ride?' she asked, as if this were an all-important criterion.

'Unfortunately not. Living in London, there isn't so much opportunity,' Frankie said.

'Bad show!' Karin was instantly sympathetic of what she saw as deep deprivation. 'I could teach you, if you like. Or Dad could, I suppose. He rides quite well.'

A faint grin touched Julian's mouth at this slightly offhanded compliment.

'Ms Somers is here to work, Karin,' he pointed out. 'Don't you have to groom Jeepers, or something?'

'I'm trying hard not to play Mr Barret of Wimpole Street,' Julian said wryly, as his daughter and her pony disappeared from sight. 'To remember that she's my child, not a member of an expedition under my leadership, which would actually be far easier to cope with. I have to keep in mind all the time that Karin is headstrong, but fairly mature. She can be led, but not pushed.'

'She seems a determined sort of girl. I would imagine that she is probably as obstinate as her father,' Frankie observed. It was a remark which, a few months ago, would have elicited an instant, tart and defensive response from him, but now he merely frowned and said mildly,

'You're very likely right. At least I know where I am with her. With Jeremy... my son... well, it's as if he has changed so much that I hardly know him any more. And I get a very definite impression he doesn't want to know *me*.'

He picked up Frankie's bag and carried it inside. More outgoing he certainly was, but the core of reserve remained an essential part of him, and she sensed him already regretting this confidence.

She had been allocated a pleasant bedroom decorated in peach and turquoise—another of Alison Tarrant's beautifully co-ordinated colour schemes, she presumed as she unpacked, taking in all the tasteful little decorative motifs and touches. For her own choice, it was all just a trifle too precious, as if it were nudging her all the time, drawing attention to the care and effort that had been lavished on it.

She wondered if perhaps Alison had had nothing much else to occupy her time? A woman who could comb the shops for exactly the right swatch of turquoise silk for pleated lamp-shades, or a tiny vase that echoed exactly the salmon-peach in the floral print curtains? Frankie had never had the leisure or the temperament for that much attention to domestic detail, and that was why her own home was an eclectic but comfortable hotch-potch of styles.

But Alison had had two children to raise, and a husband with a demanding and sometimes dangerous lifestyle. How had she managed to make Cerne Farm resemble a film set, or a magazine feature? It has nothing to do with you, she warned herself, pulling against the silken bonds of too great involvement. It had been Julian and Alison's home, just as it had been their marriage, and it must once have suited them. Where the house was concerned, it did not seem that he had made any changes.

Because he had loved her, and this was her creation, and while he still loved her, he would keep things as *she* had left them. Frankie shook out her clothes angrily and hung them up. If she were going to let herself constantly be disturbed by this sort of futile rambling, it would have been far better for her not to have come. Business, she reminded herself sternly, *that's* what you are here for. She loved Julian, that was true and inescapable, but he did not love *her*. The last thing she must do was embarrass both of them with the burden of her feelings. He did not need that.

She went down for drinks before dinner, as Julian had suggested she should, inadvertently timing her entrance just as Karin wandered in.

Julian sniffed the air.

'I'm relieved to note that you have showered, and don't smell too strongly of horse,' he said drily to his daughter, who only grinned, unperturbed. 'I don't suppose your brother has put in an appearance.'

'Oh, he's never around. He's useless. For all the company he is, I might as well be an only child,' Karin grumbled.

'You wouldn't like it if you were,' Frankie assured her, sipping Julian's extra-strong gin and tonic. 'I *was* an only child, brought up by an elderly aunt. I would have loved to have had a brother.'

'Feel free—take mine,' Karin replied fervently, wandering across to the far end of the room, where she curled up in the window seat and shut out the world beyond the earphones of her personal stereo.

'I don't think she was being intentionally rude,' Julian said a little grimly, and Frankie gave him a reassuring smile.

'It isn't rudeness. They're all like that—at least, if the children of my friends are anything to judge by,' she said.

'You seem to understand young people better than I do,' he observed. 'Wouldn't you like to have children of your own?'

Frankie all but gasped. The question was not all that intimate, by present-day standards, but it had deeply sexual implications that she found it hard to ignore, where he was concerned.

She fortified herself with a long swig of her drink before replying with quiet certainty, 'I wouldn't imagine that it was on the cards, not now. I don't have marriage in mind, and being a single parent doesn't appeal to me. Anyhow, there's my career. It's just one of those things I shall have to do without, I suppose.'

He was still looking at her, and she suddenly remembered a young woman who had left Cooper Masterman's to have a baby, and had come back to show him off to her ex-colleagues. He had been all pink toes and chubby arms and milky smells, transporting Frankie back to her young, newly married self, and the fierce desire for motherhood that had tormented her then. And Tom, staring at her, aghast, and saying, 'For God's sake,

Frankie, we daren't even think about it . . . and anyhow, I don't want to share you with some mewling brat!'

It was years since Frankie had even thought about that scene, and here she was, now, gazing at this man and slowly filling to overflowing with a fierce and entirely irrational longing.

'Anyway, I'm too old now,' she said angry with this illogical sensation, and with him for arousing it, even unwittingly.

'That's a ridiculous statement,' he scoffed with a faint smile intended to demonstrate superior male reasoning power, which annoyed her even more.

'Oh, yes? It's very easy for you to say it! Having children is great for men, at any age, because they aren't the ones who have to do it!' she exclaimed. 'Nappies and broken nights and . . . give me a break, Julian! It's not for me!' She ran out of steam, wondering who she was trying to convince, him or herself.

'I take your point. Don't glare at me so accusingly, as if I had made an improper suggestion to you,' he said wryly. 'Here, let me top up your glass.'

She allowed him to do so, although considering his tendency to serve at least doubles she wasn't sure it was wise. But anything to drown this awful, aching vision of herself having a baby—his baby. She wished he *would* make an improper suggestion to her, and she wished she had the reckless nerve to say yes to it.

Back in London, she had been strong-willed enough to insist that she would never give herself to a man who still loved someone else, and who would be only using her. Now, when he was close enough to touch once more, she was terribly afraid that she would take him any way he chose to come to her. Her best defence was that he himself, the moment of desire no more now than an embarrassing memory, would have no inclination to do so.

Watch your step, Frankie, she warned herself. A sure-fire way of revealing how strongly she felt was by over-reacting to every casual remark that he made, and wasn't that what she had just been guilty of doing?

'OK.' She forced a grin and a shrug. 'I suppose marriage and motherhood are fine in themselves, but as it happens, I like my life as it is. I'd have to be mad to reorganise it around some man and a brood of children, wouldn't I?'

'Indeed you would,' he agreed, holding her in the spotlight of his steady, quizzical regard. 'You have got everything very neatly organised, I would say. I only wish I could say the same for myself! Here I am with Karin, who only wants to be here because of the riding, and Jeremy who would rather not be here at all, and Mrs Coomer, who disappears back to the village every night after cooking dinner. I should warn you, by the way, that it won't be anything very special. She only does what she calls "plain cooking" and never seems to have that on the table when one expects it.'

There was a resigned humour in his complaint, but truth as well. Dinner that night turned out to be roast lamb, with slightly overcooked vegetables and an uninspired sauce.

'Oh, lord,' muttered Julian as they took their seats. He turned his head in the direction of the door, as a boy slid quickly into the room. 'You're late again,' he pointed out crisply, and said to Frankie, 'This is my son, Jeremy. He favours us with his presence as and when it suits him.'

The latecomer did not resemble either his father or his sister. He was slight, with dark auburn hair and greenish-brown eyes, and only the stubborn tilt of his chin proclaimed him to be Julian's son.

'I don't see how I can be late, when dinner is never on time here like it is at Mum's,' he said defiantly, glaring at his father who glared back and said,

'That's irrelevant. I expect *you* to be here at the appointed hour, especially when we have guests, and it might be considered polite if you were to say hello to Ms Somers.'

The boy remembered his manners.

'How do you do,' he said coolly, and his demeanour was a study in glacial courtesy worthy of Julian himself.

'Didn't I tell you he was a pain?' Karin said clearly to Frankie.

'That will do, Karin,' Julian said.

Oh, no, my love, this is not the way for you to win back your son, Frankie cried inwardly, her heart aching for him. As they picked their way carefully through the lacklustre meal, with small talk and barely avoided areas of conflict, it was blazingly obvious to Frankie that Jeremy's allegiance had been given unequivocally to his mother; that he saw Cerne Farm as a little kingdom from which the queen had been unjustly exiled, and that he resented any other woman's presence in it...even Frankie's, for all she had come under the unimpeachable flag of business. But she could see that the boy was suffering, and that he did not really understand why things were as they were.

Somehow, dinner was endured, and then Julian suggested that as he and Frankie had work to discuss, the young people might like to watch TV in the den. Karin acceded readily, saying that there was a pop group on tonight that she particularly liked, but Jeremy announced stiffly that he was going to read in his room.

'You don't have to tell me that I'm going about it all wrong,' Julian said as they settled down with coffee in the lounge. 'I'm aware of it, but I can't help myself, and I just don't seem able to get through on any level.'

'I don't think it's for me to interfere or even to offer advice,' she said cautiously. 'As a single, child-free woman, I'm hardly qualified. However...I'd say that Karin seems to be fairly well adjusted, and suffering from no more than normal teenage stroppiness. But...I wonder, does Jeremy actually understand fully why you and his mother split up? He seems to think it's all down to you, from his attitude.'

'You surely don't expect me to discuss it with him?' She saw a moment's incredulous pain flash across his face, and knew that whatever Alison had done, he would never descend to condemning her, or speaking ill of her to their son. 'I imagine he gathered that there was someone else in Alison's life—he isn't a fool. But he probably thought it was all my fault for neglecting her, ultimately. For not being around when I was needed.'

Because doubtless that was the story he had constantly been fed, during the time he had been under the sole influence of his mother, Frankie thought, and she all but said it. More suggestible than his sister, who had a strong streak of realism in her make-up, Jeremy had swallowed this line completely.

'But you can't let him go on believing that your absence gave her a legitimate excuse to...to play around?' she urged, low-voiced. 'And you surely don't believe it yourself?'

He shrugged.

'Who's to say? I *was* away often, and when I was here, involved in the planning stages of the next expedition, I was usually obsessive and intensely wrapped up in it. I had to be. Not only results but also lives often depended on getting it right. In the interludes between trips, I did try to unwind and live normally, but it wasn't easy, so maybe I didn't always succeed. Maybe I didn't try hard enough.'

This was more than she could take.

'But you can't blame yourself for... for what Alison did!' she cried. 'That's unfair! We are all of us responsible for our own actions, and we can't push that responsibility off on to someone else! That would be too easy!'

'Drop it, Frankie,' he said. His voice was sharp with warning, and the icy reserve had crept back into his eyes, telling her plainly that she had overstepped the mark. Lulled by his more relaxed manner, by the easing of constraint between them, she had dared to trespass on forbidden ground... the holy ground of his enduring love for this unknown woman. A love which refused to die.

'OK, I won't say any more. It's really none of my business,' she said, carefully and deliberately formal. 'Let's get back to this journal of yours. I can't tell you how pleased and excited I am that you're prepared to consider publication. I'm ready to sign up the minute you are, and to publish it as a separate entity, if you like. I'm sure Ivor Masterman would go along with that. But, as I suggested to you, it really might be better worked in as part of the whole.'

'You think it's that good?' He sounded surprised, even doubtful.

'I think it's terrific. In fact, I *know* it is. As yet, of course, no one at Cooper Masterman is even aware of its existence, but I trust my own instincts absolutely on this one. There will be no problems at that end, I assure you.'

Some warmth had come back into his eyes, and he was looking at her with a penetrating, questioning gaze.

'You kept it to yourself all these months, even when you felt strongly that I should publish,' he said. 'You didn't try to put pressure on me, or enlist anyone else to help you to do so. What did I do to deserve that much loyalty, I wonder? As I recall, I didn't treat you with any great respect or consideration.'

She gulped. I kept quiet because I cared about you far more than I cared about anything you might write, she thought. Because I loved you. But all she said, drily, was, 'Putting pressure on you, Julian, is rather like banging one's head against a brick wall. Besides, if you can't feel you can trust me, I've no business being your editor.'

'Nevertheless,' he said steadily, 'I owe you my thanks for that—and for much more. You saw, before I did, that the journal was the book I had to write. It was what the ancient Greeks called catharsis—a spiritual purging.' He gave a short, self-deprecating laugh. 'In plain Anglo-Saxon, better known as getting it out of your system.'

The room was suddenly very quiet, so hushed that Frankie was aware of the clock ticking, of her own breathing, of the inexorable passing of the minutes of her life. Catharsis? So far as his experiences in Amazonia, his injuries both of body and spirit, his forced break with his previous way of life were concerned, yes, he was over all that, she could see. But his love for his wife could not be so neatly exorcised. It went on and on, and so long as it possessed his heart and his mind Frankie could see no real hope for her.

'And... what next?' she asked gravely. 'Will you go on writing in the future, do you think?'

'In the long term, who knows?' he replied. 'For now, it was just a necessary exercise. I want to be doing again, not merely reflecting on what I have already done. The local college of higher education has been after me to do some lecturing—biology, natural sciences. I would also like to run a course for young people, passing on my knowledge of survival techniques. And above all I want to do something for those wretched Indian tribes...start a foundation to help them, mobilise public opinion.'

She laughed shakily.

'My goodness, I can see you're barely going to have a spare minute!' she said. She had no doubt that he would be formidable in each and any of these capacities. He had the energy and the resolve for all three.

So that was the end of it, or very nearly, she reasoned, lying in the strange bed that night, hearing the whispering of trees outside instead of the occasional rattle of passing trains. She would see his work through to fruition, and then, inevitably, he would pass out of her orbit. There would be no point at which his life would touch hers. But the memory of him would be with her always. She would go on loving him, if only from a distance, not because she chose to, or even wanted to, but quite simply because she did not know how to give up.

Frankie awoke very early in the morning—her watch said six o'clock—with a raging thirst, induced, most likely, by Julian's ferociously strong gin and tonics. Slipping on her robe over her nightdress, she tiptoed downstairs to the kitchen, found a glass, and was just filling it with water when a sound startled her.

Turning around, she saw Jeremy in the doorway, and it was doubtful which of them was the more surprised.

'Oh, hello,' she said. 'I was thirsty, and so I came down for a drink. What gets you up so early?'

He was wearing cycling shorts and a T-shirt, and he carried a small rucksack. Frankie smiled at him tentatively, thinking that he must have inherited his slight, fine-boned build and dark, romantic colouring from his mother. She imagined him in female form, a slim auburn-haired woman with those mysterious greenish eyes, and could not help wincing slightly. Perhaps that was what Julian found so hard to take, looking at this boy and seeing another image of the woman he loved?

'I'm going out,' he said shortly. 'For the day.'

'Oh,' she said, rather at a loss. 'I suppose the bag is full of food rations, then?'

'Some. But mostly it's full of books.' Seeing her puzzlement, he stammered on a little. 'I...er...what I do is cycle out into the country, find somewhere quiet, and...er...read.'

'What a perfectly lovely idea!' Frankie said genuinely, and the very, very faint smile told her that this boy was not really rude, just shy and hurt. 'I like to read in the park, in my lunch hour sometimes, but I don't imagine it's as peaceful as the country. Do you read a lot?'

'Loads. All the time, in fact. Didn't you know that I'm the family misfit?' he said gloomily. 'Mum likes fashion and nice things, Karin only likes horses, and my father...well...'

A mental flashback transported Frankie to the sunlit Languedoc, and Julian's study, her astounded discovery of the tough, hard man who read Wordsworth...

'I think you'll find that your father reads a lot, too,' she said quietly. 'Did you know, for instance, that he likes poetry?'

Jeremy's eyes narrowed with disbelief.

'Nah!' he said suspiciously. 'All he likes is charging off someplace and doing dangerous things. If that's what he enjoys, fine. Trouble is, now he can't do those things any more, since he hurt his leg. So he wants me to learn all that survival stuff so I can follow in his footsteps!'

'I don't think that's true,' Frankie said reasonably. 'Your father thinks that survival training would be a useful attribute for anyone to learn, but as for what he does...used to do...that was a very individualistic thing. It's not like a family business that one can inherit.'

'I know. But that's what he wants. I know he does. Mum told me so. And there's no way. *No way.* I don't want to be an explorer. I want to be...I dunno...a librarian? Or perhaps something like you do.'

'Books. I see,' Frankie said. 'But...Jeremy...perhaps you've misinterpreted your father a little, don't you think?'

The slight thaw vanished behind a freezing fog of icy withdrawal.

'I think my mother knows my father better than *you* do,' he said haughtily.

Frankie shrugged. Looks were only superficial, and this boy was more like Julian than he had yet begun to learn.

'I dare say she does. Didn't she also teach you the old saying that manners maketh man?'

He had the youth and the grace to blush.

'Sorry,' he said at once. 'I didn't mean...er...you know. Look, when you see my father, could you tell him I've gone out for the day?'

'I could,' she said. 'But it would be far better if you wrote him a note yourself.'

He stared at her for a few seconds, realised that she meant what she said, and then gave in, scribbling briefly on the pad behind the door, probably kept there for Mrs Coomer's shopping lists, and then, mumbling goodbye, he left. As she went back upstairs to her room, Frankie heard his bicycle wheels crunch over the gravel of the drive.

Sleep, now, was out of the question. She lay watching the sun grow brighter through the peach and turquoise curtains, daydreaming vainly but helplessly about an alternative life which could never be hers...a life in which she worked to heal the breach in this cruelly divided family...in which she stood by Julian's side, encouraging him in all his new endeavours, and slept in his arms at night...a life in which her love somehow turned this window-dresser's set piece into a home, and Jeremy learned to trust his father. A life in which Julian loved her. *Her* and not Alison. A life she could live only in the imagination.

She closed her eyes and tried hard to dispel this seductive chimera which could bring her nothing but the pain of the long, hard fall back to reality, and for a while, she floated in a mental limbo, although it could not have been called sleep.

It was the loud neighing of a horse that brought her fully awake again, and she peered out of her window, which was at the rear of the house, just in time to see mount and rider effortlessly clear the fence and trot across the field.

The rider was a girl of perhaps twenty or so, slim and straight-backed, in perfectly fitting jodhpurs that streamlined her slender flanks. As Frankie watched, she saw Julian emerge from the house, already fully dressed in jeans and a sports shirt. She saw the girl dismount gracefully and pull off her hard riding hat, shaking free a wealth of long, tumbled yellow curls.

Frankie had seen plenty of lithe young creatures like this in London bars, shaking their locks in everyone's drink, tossing them back like banners to attract male attention, as this one did now, taking Julian's hand to greet him, and actually standing on tiptoe to kiss his cheek. He did not rebuff this gesture, and his laughter drifted up to Frankie who thought enviously, Oh, to be sweet and twenty and to be allowed to kiss Julian Tarrant as though it were the most natural thing in the world!

At the same time as she tried to squash this senseless jealousy, there was a swift knock on her door and as she called out, 'Come in,' Karin all but burst into the room like a whirlwind.

'Can I look out of your window—I can't see the back from mine?' she demanded, running across the room and suiting actions to words. 'Yes, it is Amanda!' she squealed excitedly. 'I haven't seen her in ages, but I always used to go to her place on Sundays when I was living here. She does show-jumping and dressage, and her horses are super.'

'She's very pretty,' Frankie said.

'Isn't she? She's nice, too.' Karin giggled. 'I rather think she fancies Dad! Actually, she was one of their bridesmaids when he and Mum got married, yonks ago. Amanda was just a kid then, of course.'

She doesn't look much more, now, Frankie thought uncharitably, but that wasn't true, she admitted a moment later. Amanda was a very lovely young woman, well-equipped in all the right places. She had youth and energy, shared Julian's background, and at least one of his children liked her. According to Karin, she had a *tendresse* for him. One day, if he ever woke up and decided the time had come to put his love for Alison behind him, Amanda would make him a very acceptable second wife.

'I think I'll get dressed and go over to Amanda's,' Karin said eagerly. 'I'll tell Dad, first. He won't mind, I'm sure.'

Frankie watched the blonde girl remount, waving cheerily to Julian, and take the fence again as if it were nothing—as it would be for a seasoned show-jumper— and a few minutes later, she saw Karin trot off, mounted on Jeepers.

She sighed and wondered whether she should now dress and go downstairs. It was eight o'clock and the household was astir, Sunday morning or not. Perhaps she could make a pot of tea for Julian and herself, she thought, amazed by the absurd pleasure she derived at the idea of performing this simple task, and sharing a moment of domesticity with him.

'Frankie!'

His voice calling her from the foot of the stairs was too imperative to be ignored, and she raked her fingers swiftly through her hair before emerging on to the landing.

'Good morning.' Not since those seemingly long ago days in France had they awoken in the same place, and even then, by the time she saw him, she had been dressed and tidy, not clad in a skimpy silk nightdress with shoe-string straps, over which she had hastily slipped her arms into her robe.

He stood with a hand resting on the newel post, looking up at her, his annoyed expression putting paid to her dreams of a brief domestic idyll.

'I can't find Jeremy anywhere,' he said. 'Have you seen him, or heard him about? He doesn't appear to be in the house.'

It was hardly her responsibility, so why did she feel so apprehensive?

'I did see him, much earlier, when I happened to come down for a glass of water,' she said. 'He left a note——'

Clutching the robe around her, she negotiated the stairs, aware as she passed him of several conflicting and disturbing impressions. Waves of irritation flowing from him, an unmistakable concern mingled with his annoyance. The clean warmth of his body which made her feel, as always, fragile and vulnerable, and at the same time possessed of a vibrant inner power.

She fetched the note from the kitchen and handed it to him, a little nervously.

'Gone out—back later,' he read, in a faintly scornful voice. 'Well, now, that's what I would call highly informative, wouldn't you? A few more details would have been helpful, such as where he has gone, and how much later he intends coming home.'

His stinging tone caused Frankie to draw herself up, holding herself erect, as if that would give her dignity, despite her deshabille.

'I didn't actually read what he wrote,' she said. She forbore to add that, had she not happened to encounter him by chance, the boy would have been gone without so much as a word of explanation.

'It didn't occur to you to ask him where the hell he was going, running off in the early hours?' He screwed up the note, letting it flutter to the ground, and folded his arms, glaring accusingly at Frankie, as if it were entirely her fault that he was constantly at loggerheads with his son.

'I didn't need to ask him, as a matter of fact,' she said, icily defensive. 'He volunteered the information. He's gone out on his bike, with a bag full of books to read. I would have thought that *you*, of all people, would have understood the need to get out and be on one's own. You did enough of it, as I recall. Can't you allow him the same space?'

'So now you know my son better than I do, after a few hours' acquaintance,' he said sardonically, the old, bitter smile twisting his mouth. 'Got all the answers, haven't you, Frankie—to your own life and everyone else's!'

'I don't know why you're taking this out on me!' she retorted. 'But yes—if you want my opinion, if you let that boy go on believing you'd like him to follow in your footsteps professionally, then you're asking for trouble!'

'Don't be ridiculous!' he said scornfully. 'Why on earth should I have any such expectations? That would be foolish. It's obviously not for him, and if you think I would go in for that kind of compensation simply because my own expedition days are over, then you're being damned insulting!'

Half a metre of bristling space was all that separated them, now. His eyes were blazing with outrage, and Frankie was incandescent with anger, because she was taking the fall-out from a problem for which another woman—his beloved, precious Alison—was totally responsible.

'It isn't what I think—it's what *Jeremy* thinks!' she flung at him. 'It's what his mother has been force-feeding him, along with all that other rubbish about the break-up being entirely your fault.'

She saw his head jerk upwards, his jaw tighten in stubborn refusal to believe so much malice could exist in a woman he loved, who had once loved him, and she flung out her hands in despair.

'I give up! You were man enough to risk your own life for your party! You were man enough to fight your way back through injury and stress, and to put that experience on paper for others to learn from. So why can't you be man enough to stop letting Alison dictate the course of your life from a distance? Or is that too much to ask of yourself?'

Tears stinging her eyes, she turned and half stumbled back up the stairs, snatching at her trailing robe to prevent herself from tripping and losing the last remnants of her dignity. An ominous silence followed her as she closed her bedroom door behind her and stood staring out of her window with blank, unseeing eyes, arms hugging herself protectively, head bent.

Less than a minute passed before she heard the door open again, and knew he was in the room. He stood behind her, so close she could feel his breath ruffling her hair at the crown, but still she did not turn.

'Frankie.' His voice was quiet, but charged with purpose. 'You can't level that kind of accusation against me any longer without taking the consequences. You know that, don't you?'

'Go away, Julian. Leave me alone,' she begged woodenly. It was hopeless. He loved Alison, she knew it, but she loved *him*. She did not want to love him any more fiercely, to be in any deeper than she already was.

'Not a chance,' he said, and taking her by the shoulders, turned her round. She saw the dark shadows of desire around his eyes, and felt it in his urgent fingers as he pushed the robe from her shoulders. She was suddenly afraid, recognising a force in him, and in herself, that was too strong for her to handle.

'No,' she said instinctively. 'No...no...'

He only laughed and ignored her protests. He tilted her chin back with one firm hand, and his mouth claimed hers, persuasive, invading, accepting no refusal, simply taking what he wanted, without asking or needing her permission.

And indeed, by then he no longer required it, because she had stopped fighting him, stopped fighting herself. Thought had fled, reason was suspended, and there was only the driving need she no longer knew how to deny. This was the man she wanted, and this the fate that had stalked her relentlessly since the day she met him. She wound her arms round his neck as he lifted her easily on to the bed, shivering with an unconcealed impatience that matched his own as he peeled the nightdress clean to her waist with one swift movement.

It had been too long in the waiting to be gentle, and she exploded with answering desire as soon as his hands touched her. He took her by storm, swiftly, urgently, and the passion in him was so strong she felt her whole body aching with the impact of it. Drawing him deeper and deeper into her, coiling herself round him, crying out and biting into his back with her nails, she gave and gave unconditionally, and took in return, not submissive in her surrender, but fierce and splendid until the final shattering moment.

'At last!' he exclaimed, and that was all he said until they were lying side by side, drenched in perspiration and smiling gravely at each other like two unrepentant sinners.

It was a while before she could speak, she was so replete with turbulent emotion, and even longer before she could find any words to express half of what she was feeling. Not even daring to venture on such a task, she fell back on flippancy.

'My God!' she gasped finally. 'A woman has to watch what she says to you, in case you take it as a challenge!'

He rolled over swiftly, making light of the energy he had so lately and vigorously expended, and propped himself on one elbow to look down searchingly into her face.

'And wasn't it?'

'No.' She shook her head firmly, tracing her fingers up his bronzed chest, unable to keep from touching him. 'I told you before, you never had anything to prove. Not in that sense. I never had the slightest doubts about your...virility. Not for one minute.'

'But *I* did.' He smiled faintly. The admission came hard, and, contrarily, she knew a lesser man could not have made it. 'For a long time, I did. It was you who made me realise I wasn't quite dead and completely useless. That's yet another thing I have to thank you for, Frankie.'

She could have wept then. Lying there, looking up at this man she loved, with all she desired within her reach, but in reality as far away as ever, she supressed a wave of deep anguish and forced a light smile.

'Manuscripts read and considered, male egos restored!' she quipped facetiously. 'Julian—it wasn't a gift. It was something that happened—something we both wanted. Or so I thought.'

'That you can't doubt,' he said. 'The first afternoon you sat here in this house, I looked at you and found myself wondering how you would look naked. I didn't want to think about you, or any woman, that way, at that time. But it's the truth.'

'You shock me, sir! I thought you only wanted to be let alone, like Greta Garbo.' She grinned. Light, Frankie, keep it light, she warned herself inwardly. It's only your body he wants, remember, not your heart and your immortal soul. So play it very cool...

Outside, the morning sun rose high and bright in the sky over Cerne Farm, and the birds made an infernal racket in the tall trees. But Frankie was oblivious to the world outside as Julian made love to her again, slowly, this time, and with an exquisite, leisured thoroughness that left every inch of her glowing with serene fulfilment. She thought she would burst and overflow with pleasure and happiness, and with the strange sorrow which ran like a dark current beneath it.

AN EASY MAN TO LOVE 157

For how long could she pretend that for her, as for him, this was not love, only a clamouring physical hunger?

How long did she have?

CHAPTER NINE

KARIN did not return from her visit to Amanda's until two o'clock, and by that time there was nothing to indicate that her father and his editor had spent the morning in bed together.

Except, perhaps, that Julian was in a remarkably cheerful mood, and Frankie's eyes, her skin, her entire being shone with an inner glow that lifted her from an attractive woman into the realms of real beauty, but thirteen-year-old minds would not have been capable of the connecting link that could have strung these isolated perceptions together.

'It's Mrs Coomer's day off,' Julian had told Frankie as he finally hauled her out of bed. 'She doesn't work Sundays. It's fend-for-ourselves day, so before we investigate what the kitchen holds, I'm going in the shower, and so are you.'

'No way—not together!' she exclaimed aghast, and he grinned.

'Come on, Frankie, you can't be shy—look at you, you haven't a stitch on right this minute, and very enticing you look, if I might say so.'

'I'm not shy.' Nevertheless, she grabbed her robe and pulled it on. 'But if you and I shower together, there's only one way it will end, and you know it!'

He smiled down at her with subtle, powerful suggestiveness.

'You mean you might be tempted to have your wicked way with me all over again?' he murmured. 'Underwater? That sounds very interesting, I must say! What are we waiting for?'

She made a swift attempt to slip past him, but he grabbed hold of her arm in a reflex action too fast to avoid, and drew her close again, kissing her long and thoroughly.

'Ah...Julian,' she sighed, and very, very regretfully eased away from him. 'Don't we have to think about food? And what if Karin should come back?'

'You weren't worrying about either, five minutes ago,' he reminded her, but he did let her go. 'All right—I'll behave if you insist. Ladies first.'

No, she hadn't been worrying about anything, Frankie admitted soberly as she stepped into the shower and turned the jets full on. For the last two hours she had not thought at all; nothing had existed outside the two of them, and the way he had made her feel.

It was as if...as if they were the first man and woman on earth to take and use this immense, awesome power for themselves. Frankie had never denied that making love was pleasurable, but that was an inadequate word to describe the primeval surrender of herself to another, the forgetting and finding of herself in an act of such beauty and potency. This was not something she could just go home and forget, or remember fondly. It had changed her essentially, where she really counted, and she would never be the same.

What am I going to do? she asked herself helplessly, towelling her wet hair and staring at her wide-eyed reflection materialising in the steamed-up mirror. I can't live without him, not for a day. I'll die. I'll stop breathing. Something vital will seize up and refuse to work.

But the bleak truth was that she had to. The best she could hope for was that this was a beginning—that he would go on wanting her, and that through his desire she might find a secret way into his life. The real fear that she faced this morning was that even if she did find such a way, it would prove to be a dead end. She would come slap up against the brick wall of his love for Alison, beyond which she could not penetrate. He would allow her in only so far, and she wanted all of him.

Frankie summoned up all her considerable inner reserves of strength and optimism in order not to destroy or spoil what she already had. While Julian was in the shower, she tidied her bed—if she left it in this state for Mrs Coomer to find tomorrow, half of Dorset would know what had taken place—then she slipped into jeans and a shirt and went down to the kitchen.

By the time he joined her, she had made tea and toast, discovered there was a chicken in the fridge, jointed it and prepared it for a casserole.

'What a double pleasure—a woman in the kitchen as well as in the bedroom,' he said, smiling with perfect male satisfaction. 'And this one just happens to be an excellent editor as well! What more could I ask for?'

She pulled a face at him.

'Flattery will get you a long way, but it won't get you off scot-free. I need someone to peel potatoes,' she informed him prosaically.

'Oh, Frankie——' The slow shake of his head was not refusal, but rather a kind of puzzlement. 'You, lady, are something else, as my offspring might rather sloppily express it!'

Because she wasn't already wringing her hands with *angst* over whether she should have slept with him or not? Because she appeared to have taken the whole thing in the same spirit that he had, as a matter of an intense hunger they had very pleasurably satisfied? Wasn't that the kind of woman he had imagined her to be all along— urbane, sensual but emotionally detached, too mature to make a fuss over what was an entirely natural function?

That should make it easier for her to play the part, she reflected as she chopped onions and carrots, and with luck she need not betray too many hints of how she really felt about him. She dared not risk making him retreat once more behind his private barricade and pull up the drawbridge behind him.

Today had happened. Anger might have lit the blue touch paper, but it had been slow-burning for a long time, and neither of them could have prevented the ultimate explosion. But there was one thing she knew intuitively about Julian Tarrant. A relationship, however brief, on equal terms was something he might accept, but an innate decency would not allow him to make love to a woman who was involved with him over and beyond what he was able to give to her in return. If he found out that she loved him, he would probably draw a line under the whole thing, for her good as well as his own. So if she wanted the relationship to continue... and she had to admit that she did... it was vital that he did not learn that she was seriously in love with him.

She could not control the impulse to smile back when she caught his eyes resting on her with something oddly tender in them, or the need to touch him as she passed, sometimes making it appear accidental. But she could and must bite her tongue on the urge to blurt out, 'Oh, God, I love you, Julian—I love you more than I can endure!'

There was one thing, though, that she felt she must say, while they were still alone and he was in a responsive mood, something that nagged at her and troubled her, and which she could not shirk, for all he might not like it.

'Julian,' she said, 'will you promise me something?'

He looked at her, his blue eyes deeply thoughtful.

'If it's in my power, and within reason—yes.'

'Talk to Jeremy. About this notion he thinks you've got about his future.'

When he did not immediately answer, she swallowed hard and went on, 'However he's got hold of the idea, it surely can't help anything for him to think you are determined to force him into a mould he won't fit.'

He was silent for so long that she half expected the old anger to well up and overflow. But in the end, he said levelly, 'I expect it's all a misunderstanding of something that's been said, but I'll make it clear where I stand on the matter. Will that make you happy?'

It will have to do, she thought resignedly, aware that he was still refusing to accept that Alison might deliberately have sown the seeds of this dissension, and, given that, there might be others that she would attempt to plant, once she had her son back under her roof and her influence.

Love truly was blind, Frankie reflected wryly. Alison had the cake, and left me with the crumbs.

And yet . . . no, she pondered, surprising herself with the depth of the insight which suddenly came to her. For Alison perhaps did not know the man her husband had become. If he were strong before, how much stronger was he now, how much more complex, more complete in himself, having endured the experiences he had, and come out the other side? This was the man Frankie loved, she was grateful for it, and she had no regrets.

'This,' said Karin, smacking her lips over the last of the chicken, 'is much better than anything we usually have here. Jeremy will kick himself for having missed the best meal of the week! Serves him right for taking off!'

They all laughed. The atmosphere around the table had been pleasantly relaxed, almost congenial. Frankie too wished that Jeremy could have been there to share it, and perhaps he would have unbent a little.

She served up a chocolate gâteau she had found in the depths of the freezer and defrosted, then put on the coffee-pot.

'Thanks for a brill meal, Ms Somers,' Karin said, pushing back her chair.

'Oh, please—Frankie will do,' she laughed. 'Otherwise I'll feel at least ninety!'

Out of the corner of her eyes she saw Julian's carefully raised eyebrows, and felt herself blushing more like a girl of nineteen at the recollection of their passionately spent morning. She had not acted as if she were ninety then, and a wave of retrospective pleasure seized her. She wanted to be back in his arms, feeling him inside her and all around her. Now. But it couldn't be, and she did not know how she could bear to wait until once again it could.

'Is it all right if I go now, Dad?' Karin asked her father. 'Don't forget that you promised me we could go sailing in Poole Harbour one day. It's ages since we had the boat out.'

'I hadn't forgotten, but don't *you* forget that I've got work to do, or Frankie will be after my blood,' he said. 'Scoot off, now, and let us...er...geriatrics finish our coffee in peace.'

Alone with Frankie, he reached across the table and closed his hand over hers.

'I feel about as far from geriatric as it's possible to be,' he said, his voice low and charged with sincerity. 'I feel rejuvenated...reborn.'

Frankie's throat closed up with emotion, and for a moment she could not speak. He's only talking about sex, she reminded herself sternly, about the resurgence of a vital masculine drive Alison's defection had temporarily robbed him of. That's all.

'I feel pretty good, too,' she said calmly. 'But we'd better not let your daughter catch us holding hands, or she'll start asking awkward questions. And, Julian—while I am obviously keen to see this book of yours finished, it's important for you to take time out to be with your children.'

'Is this my slave-driver of an editor speaking?' he teased gently. 'You have my solemn word that I shall get to grips with the final chapters...and with my son, too, if it's humanly possible.'

They walked out into the garden, across the field to the paddock where Karin's pony grazed, and leaned over the fence together, shoulders touching only lightly. She felt the contact in every part of her body.

Beyond the cultivated lushness of the farm, the heath began, a vast, indefinite, formless world of brush, gorse, rough grass and stunted trees. It stretched away for miles,

desolate and untamed, threatening even in bright sun-
light—a wilderness in microcosm.

Julian surveyed it contentedly, like a monarch repos-
sessing a fief to which he had been born, then, turning
to Frankie, he said, 'Would you come down again next
weekend?'

'You mean—to work on the book with you?'

'No. Because I want to see you again.'

'You do?' Her own voice was studiedly level and
undemanding.

'Of course I do. Damn it, Frankie——' He dug his
fingers into her shoulders and kissed her swiftly but
fiercely. 'Come on Friday night.'

'If you like.' She remained still, gazing up at him,
conscious of a glad warmth spreading through her. He
wanted to see her! 'But what's so special about Friday?'

'Not a thing. Except that, fairly obviously, it's sooner
than Saturday,' he pointed out, 'and I'm not a patient
man.'

Frankie nursed these words to her all the way back to
London on the slow train that stopped at every small
station along the line. They meant more to her than any
eloquent protestations of poetic devotion she could have
heard from the lips of others, because they signified that,
far from merely having satisfied a one-off physical urge,
Julian was anxious to be with her again. To make love
to her, yes, and she wanted that too, with an impatience
bordering on indecency. But surely there was more?
Surely she answered a need in him that was not only
sexual? A need for her presence, her opinion, her argu-
mentative spirit as well as her body. She was beginning
to believe that need existed, and it was a beginning.

With Julian's permission she had taken his journal back with her, and on Monday morning she was able to bounce confidently into Ivor's office with the air of one who had just brought off a coup. He sent for her later in the day, and although it was not in his nature to enthuse, or to praise too fulsomely, she could see he was impressed.

'How long have you known Tarrant was writing this?' he demanded.

'Since I went to see him in France.' Ivor was too sharp to try and fool. 'But he was adamant then that he wouldn't publish, and he isn't the kind of man you can bulldoze, or even cajole into doing anything against his will.'

'Hm.' Ivor regarded her meditatively. 'So you planted the seed and waited for it to bear fruit of its own accord. Clever of you. It doesn't always work, but this time you pulled it off. Now tell me, as you did when I first suggested it, that I assigned this job to the wrong editor.'

She grinned. 'You only want me to agree that you're always right. I don't want to make you a megalomaniac.'

'I'm already a megalomaniac,' he said with a certain relish. 'However, I wouldn't dream of taking Julian Tarrant out of your capable hands at this stage, so put yourself at his disposal.'

Leaving his office, she reflected on the aptness of his words and wondered, in view of the earlier rumours, just how much he suspected, or had slyly guessed, about her relationship with this particular author. Even if he had divined the truth, he wasn't one to let it worry him, Frankie thought wryly. If the end result was a good book, Ivor wouldn't give a brass farthing what was going on behind the scenes.

Right now, ironically, she was flavour of the month at Cooper Masterman, but the reality was that she had done little to deserve the accolade. *Julian* had come to his own conclusions, without her help, without her persuasion, and even if her decision to stand back and not to press the matter had influenced him at all, she could claim no credit for it. It had not been a cleverly calculated move, but a simple human response, the motive of which had been her love for him.

For a few days, Frankie was supremely happy. Her career star was rising high. She loved Julian, and she no longer cared if people found out about their relationship. While she was not about to broadcast it from the rooftops, neither did she see why she should make an issue of denying it. They were both free and over twenty-one, and what they did together was no one's business but their own.

On Wednesday morning, she was in the process of getting ready to go to work when the telephone rang in the hall. Barefoot, hairbrush in hand, she hurried down the stairs to answer it, never expecting to hear Julian's voice.

'Frankie. Bear with me—I need to talk to someone.' He sounded wry and harrassed.

'Julian.' She conjured up her calmest voice to disguise the wild thudding of her heart, which sounded so loudly in her own ears, she was afraid that he must be able to hear it.

'It's Karin—she's injured herself,' he told her, and, hearing her anxious gasp, added quickly, 'It's not that serious. She's going to be just fine.'

'What happened?' she demanded, and could virtually hear his rueful grin as he told her.

'Karin and one of the girls from the village went out on the heath on their own. It's always been forbidden territory for my kids because I know—having grown up here myself—how deceptively dangerous it can be. There's plenty of more accessible countryside for walking or riding. On the heath, it's all too easy to get lost, which is exactly what they did.'

Frankie groaned.

'Oh, heavens, Julian—you must have been so worried,' she sympathised. 'How did she manage to hurt herself?'

'It got late, they were stumbling around in the dark, and slipped into a gully,' he said. 'The other girl sprained her ankle, and Karin has two cracked ribs. OK, she was doing something she had been expressly told not to do, but all the same, she was in my care, and I let her endanger and injure herself. What kind of a father does that make me?'

Frankie emitted a sharp laugh.

'A normal, fallible one,' she said briskly. 'You didn't *let* her do it. She went out and did it herself. Kids of that age will get up to tricks, and you can't watch them every minute of every day. Or perhaps she's a chip off the old block, with the exploring instincts in her blood! Julian, when are you going to stop blaming yourself for everything that goes wrong, or doesn't work out? You aren't master of the universe. It isn't all your responsibility.'

There was an almost palpable silence while he wrestled with this concept, and Frankie could feel, even at a distance, a wave of something like relief emanating from him.

'You reckon?' he said, surprised. 'You don't know how good it feels to hear you say that. I knew I could rely on you to give me a metaphorical kick in the pants. But I still have problems, Frankie. I don't know what to do. I'm stuck here with a teenage girl who is laid up and terminally bored. We have played Scrabble, Monopoly and Trivial Pursuit until I'm blue in the face, and Karin has worn out the video recorder, complaining that all the films we have are boring, and she's seen them all before, anyhow.'

It occurred briefly to Frankie to wonder where the hell Alison was in her daughter's hour of need, but she did not think that introducing this subject would serve any useful purpose. Instead, she looked at her watch and consigned today's schedule at Cooper Masterman to the back burner. Her place was at Cerne Farm with this re-served, oddly driven man she had come to love.

'Hang on in there. I'm on my way,' she said. 'We may not have much in the way of countryside where I live, but we are awash with good video shops who are sure to know exactly what girls of that age like to watch.'

'But Frankie . . . aren't you busy? You can't just drop everything,' he demurred.

'Watch me,' she said. 'Don't worry about it. I can't put a foot wrong at Cooper Masterman at the moment, and since it's your journal that's responsible for my exalted status, I think they can spare me for a day!'

In minutes she had rung the office, leaving a message on her answerphone for Sally, when she arrived, to cancel all her appointments for the day, and organised a hire car for herself. She drove steadily, stopping only for a cup of coffee and a sandwich at Ringwood, on the edge of the New Forest, and was negotiating the country roads leading to Canford Tarrant later that morning.

As she parked the car on the drive, Julian came out of the front door to greet her. He was calm and composed, but she did not need him to tell her that he was glad she was here. He took both her hands in his, and although he did not kiss her, the tightness of his grip sent signals racing along her nerves.

'You are as welcome as the relief of Mafeking,' he said.

'I've brought loads of films, tapes of pop music, and magazines,' she said. 'All of them are guaranteed teenage-friendly. There should be plenty here that will help to keep Karin entertained.'

'You are a miracle worker,' he said gratefully, 'in every possible way.'

For a moment they stood looking at one another, and Frankie's heart sang with happiness and hope, because his smile, that wonderful smile that could melt stone, was only for her, and he was gazing down at her as if she were the one person in the world he really wanted to see.

She forced a level, sensible, understated reaction, although what she really wanted to do was to throw herself into his arms.

'I do my humble best,' she said. 'How about putting the kettle on while I go and see the invalid.'

Karin was spreadeagled on the sofa in the den; she smiled at Frankie with her usual cheeriness, but beyond her injured ribs, which would quickly heal with the wonderful regenerative powers of youth, it was easy to see that she had had a very frightening experience.

'Well, this is going to mess up your summer holidays a little,' Frankie said sympathetically. 'Is it still painful?'

'A bit,' she confessed. 'The doctor says I'll soon be able to get around. Not that it will make much difference. Dad has grounded me until further notice.'

Frankie laughed. 'Never mind. You'll get over it. The main thing is that you are safe. It amazes me that you managed to find your way home at all, you with your broken ribs and your friend with her sprained ankle.'

Karin stared at her.

'But we couldn't. We didn't,' she said. 'We were just stuck out there, and there was nothing we could do. It was Dad who rescued us. Didn't he tell you?'

'No, he didn't,' Frankie sighed. But he wouldn't would he? her mind translated promptly. 'Do you feel like telling me about it, as that's the only way I'm ever going to get the story!'

Karin shuddered at the memory, but in the warmth and safety of Cerne Farm, the ordeal behind her, she was more than prepared to relive the drama.

'We were going round and round in circles trying to find our way home, but everywhere looked just the same,' she related with grim relish. 'It was awful, especially after it got dark, and then it started to rain. We sort of fell into this ditch, and Sarah did her foot, and I could hardly breathe. We were out there for simply ages—well, perhaps not, but it seemed like ages to us. We thought we'd be out there all night. Then Dad and Jeremy came and found us.'

She was well launched on her story now, and ready to extract the utmost attention from her audience.

'We couldn't walk, either of us, so Dad sent Jeremy home to get help. I thought Jeremy would be terrified, on his own, but he just sort of went, without arguing or anything. Then Dad made a shelter with brushwood and his waterproof coat, for us. Did you know that if you dig down a bit, there's nearly always enough dry growth, even if it's raining.'

Frankie shook her head.

'Well, it's true—Dad said so. Then he made another small shelter and built a pile of stones and made a fire out of sticks and pine cones—not under *our* shelter, because that would have smoked us out, but near enough to dry our clothes. We could only risk a fire at all because of the damp conditions, because if it had been dry, we'd have set the whole heath on fire,' Karin continued knowledgeably. 'You should always have a working cigarette lighter on you if you're out in the wilds. Dad does, even though he doesn't smoke. Then you can make a fire. He had chocolate, as well. That's a good thing to have. And he strapped me up and made a temporary splint for Sarah's ankle. We had to tear up clothes for that. I never realised Dad knew all that stuff!'

Frankie was a little dazed as she went in search of tea, which she found in the kitchen, freshly brewed by Julian. He raised his eyebrows at the bemused expression on her face.

'As you see, she is all in one piece, and the experience hasn't affected her powers of speech,' he said drily.

'Indeed it hasn't. But it's thanks to you that she's safe and sound,' she said. 'You didn't tell me that, did you, but your daughter has spent the last ten minutes regaling me with survival techniques.'

'It's no big deal, Frankie,' he said quietly. 'I know the heath, and have known it all my life. As for survival, in those circumstances, it's a matter of basic first-aid, making yourselves as comfortable as possible, and waiting for help to come. Luckily I had taken Jeremy along, so while I set about looking after the girls he was able to go back and fetch help.'

'And you trusted him to be able to make his way back alone in the dark, and do so?' Frankie observed. The shy, bookish boy who would have had no idea how to splint limbs or do whatever else was necessary to prevent his sister and her friend from suffering the ill effects of injury and exposure had none the less risen to the occasion magnificently, and played his part.

'He's *my* son, after all. Why shouldn't I trust him?' Julian said, looking at her as if she had overlooked something vital and obvious. And that said it all, she thought.

'That's very true,' she said gravely. 'When the chips were down, you didn't hesitate to call on him. If he realises that too, Julian, you are more than halfway towards a better understanding.'

Frankie spent the rest of the day at Cerne Farm, talking and playing games with Karin. Finally, when the girl had dozed off on the sofa, she said, 'I ought to be going now, Julian. It's a long drive back.'

'You *could* stay here tonight,' he pointed out, his hand resting on her shoulder, fingers lightly rubbing over her collarbone and moving up towards her throat. She stifled a moan. It would be so easy to say yes, and she knew that if she did she would end up in his arms. She wanted this more than she could say, and it was with mammoth self-denial that she shook her head.

'I can't—I have a publicity meeting first thing in the morning that I can't afford to miss,' she groaned.

'Obviously, that must take priority,' he said with a flash of the old, dry sarcasm she remembered so well, but now, instead of annoying her, it filled her with a burgeoning hope. If he resented the claims her job made on her, then surely, it must mean that he wanted her... mustn't it?

'You'll be here on Friday night,' he said at the very last minute, just as she was about to get into the driver's seat.

It wasn't a question. Nor was there any longer the pretext of his needing her to help with his book. Purely and simply, he wanted her to be with him, and she wanted it too. There was no point in pretending otherwise.

'I'll be there,' she confirmed without hesitation, and although they did not kiss it was implicit in the air around them.

Frankie floated through the next day on Cloud Nine, and on Friday morning, before leaving for work, she put through a quick call to Cerne Farm to tell Julian the time of her train.

It was Karin who answered.

'Dad's out in the garden,' she said. 'I'll hobble to the door and give him a call, if you like.' She hesitated, and then went on, 'Frankie... I want to ask you something.'

'Ask away.'

'It's...' Again the hesitation, and then all in a rush, she said, 'Do you think if people split up, and then get back together again, can it work out?'

Frankie's heart missed a beat, and a peculiar sensation came over her.

'I suppose it can, sometimes,' she said slowly. 'It all depends. Who do you have in mind, Karin?'

'Why, Mum and Dad, of course,' the girl said as if that were self-evident. 'My mum wants to come back. She talked to Dad on the phone yesterday... I didn't hear what they said...but she talked to me, and it's true...they're getting back together.'

'Are you sure about this, Karin?' Frankie heard herself saying numbly, and it was as if her own voice were coming from very far away. 'I thought...' warily, seeking how to express this to a thirteen-year-old '...I thought your mum had a new boyfriend.'

'She did. But that's all over now. I'm...I'm a bit nervous about them being together again, but it will be all right, won't it? They *are* my mum and dad, after all. Frankie? Are you still there? Shall I call Dad for you now?'

'No, don't do that,' Frankie said quickly. 'I have to go now, Karin. I'll ring later...'

No! No! No! She put down the phone and leaned, shaking, over it. It isn't true! It can't be true! She was gutted, flayed and disembowelled, but deep inside her she did not question it, for wasn't it what she had known and feared all along? Hadn't she always been afraid that he wasn't hers, and these last few bright days had been no more than an illusion...which was now over and finished? Ahead lay nothing but darkness.

CHAPTER TEN

SHE got through the morning on automatic pilot, doing everything she had to do precisely and mechanically, intent merely on surviving, and not allowing herself the indulgent luxury of thought. And as the day wore on, her misery began to change, subtly but surely, into a black, desperate anger.

How could he do this to her? How could he? All the time he had been working, moving towards a reconciliation with Alison, he had allowed Frankie to get closer to him . . . he had taken her and made love to her, until now she was deeply and irretrievably in love with him, bound to him . . . and it did not mean a thing. She wanted to scream with the pain of loss, the knife-wound of bitter deception. It hurt, hurt, hurt, and she did not know how to contain it, or how to let it loose.

But wait. Julian had not truly deceived her, because he had never, ever promised her anything. Never led her to believe he loved her, or ever would. All he had done was to desire her, as she had made it equally plain she had desired him. What they had done was what they had both wanted to do, and she had carefully hidden her love for him, convinced that had he been aware of it, nothing would ever have happened between them. It was just an affair. It had passed the time pleasurably, and it had given him back his sexual self-respect. As for her, he thought she was a woman of the world, who probably did this sort of thing all the time, for all she had denied it.

Yes, perhaps he could have told her that moves were afoot towards getting back together with Alison, but maybe he had simply considered it to be bad form to discuss one woman while sexually involved with another. There had been plenty of markers along the route, which she had read accurately, and ignored nevertheless. Julian had never denied that he still loved Alison. It had been clear to Frankie from the outset, and, knowing it, she had gone ahead. Could she now turn around and blame anyone but herself?

There was one thing left for her to do, and when she could put it off no longer, she said, in what she hoped were normal tones, 'Sally, will you get me Julian Tarrant on the phone, please?' Then she shut her office door and retreated behind her desk, waiting, numb with a self-induced mental anaesthesia.

It wore off the instant she heard his voice, and she was hurting again, unbearably.

'Frankie.' His tone was lazy, full of a seductive appeal, sure of her, sure of himself. She hated him. Hated her own gullibility. 'Karin said you had phoned earlier but had to rush off, so I assumed you had a busy schedule at the office?'

'Yes. I'm extremely busy.' She spread her hand below her heart, trying to ease the pain she had never realised could be so gut-wrenchingly physical. 'In fact . . . Julian, about this weekend. I shan't be coming down after all. I'm sorry.'

There, she had said it. Curtly, and in a rush, before she could give in to the urge to see him, hold him, be with him one more time.

'Oh? And why not?' He must have picked up something from the coldness of her manner. She had tried to keep her voice neutral and free from emotion, but it was more than she could do to bite on her misery completely.

'I just think it would be better if I didn't,' she said tautly. 'I would prefer it if we could keep our relationship strictly professional from now on. Can we leave it at that?'

'If you don't see fit to explain your sudden attack of reluctance, then I don't see how or why I can compel you to do so,' he said, equally cold. 'If that's all you think I deserve by way of explanation, then so be it.'

It's more than you thought *I* deserved, she wanted to shout at him, but she could not, dared not get into an emotional slanging match, or she would probably start crying and accusing, and then he would know how she felt. And what good could that possibly do now? It would only make her feel even worse, as she threw out her dignity along with her heart.

'Very well then. Goodbye,' she said, and slammed down the phone abruptly. He wasn't going to press her more strongly for a reason for her change of mind, which only went to show, she thought bleakly, how little it mattered to him. She was just a woman he had enjoyed taking to bed, and very soon he would have his true heart's desire back with him.

Frankie was not about to plead or weep or bombard him with recriminations about his misuse of her, if it could be so called. Such as it was, the affair was over. She had been a fool to let it begin, and she could only pray that by the time she was obliged to see him again on business she would have got a firm grip on herself.

Frankie dragged herself through what remained of the day, making all the necessary decisions at work, talking and smiling at people as normally as possible, even though it was all false.

She knew she had to learn this technique, and learn it well, because the need for it was not going to go away. The sun would rise and set, season would follow season, and Julian would still not be hers. She wouldn't drown in his smile, or bridle under the whip of his cool sarcasm, she wouldn't feel the touch of his hand, or the stimulating *frisson* of his mind engaging hers. All that was lost to her. Would it hurt less, with time? Frankie did not know, and she could only hope.

She could see that Sally was not fully deceived by her act.

'You've been on top of the world for the last few days, and since you made that phone call to Julian Tarrant you've been as if you're playing a part in a film or something. Not quite real,' she said. 'You're in love with him, aren't you? I've suspected it for some time. Can't you simply tell him this?'

Frankie did not trouble to deny it.

'That's the last thing I can do,' she said dully. 'He wouldn't want to know. He's getting back together with his ex-wife. To be honest, I don't think he ever really believed in the reality of the divorce, even though he initiated it.'

'I'm sorry, Frankie,' Sally said compassionately. 'It sounds a foolhardy thing to do, expecting it to work out the second time around. And somehow, he doesn't come across as a fool.'

Frankie sniffed miserably.

'Love makes fools of us all,' she said bitterly. 'He's a tough, clever, very able man, but she has him right where she wants him. If he loves her that much, there's nothing more to be said.'

Saturday morning found Frankie hunched over the breakfast bar in her kitchen, drinking coffee and flipping idly through the pages of the *Independent*. She was wearing her oldest jeans, frayed at the hems and patched rather than fashionably ripped, and a shirt almost ready to be consigned to the next local jumble sale, because she had promised herself that this morning she would muck out the garden shed. It needed doing, but then, it had needed doing for some time, only now she had decided grimly that a spasm of hard, unpleasant manual work would be good for her. It would be therapeutic, and would prevent her from dwelling morbidly on her heartbreak. If anything could.

One more cup of coffee, she told herself, and then I'll stop putting it off, and get on with it before the sun gets too hot for comfort. And then perhaps she would stop thinking about where she had hoped to be this morning— waking up at Cerne Farm, in Julian's arms.

She went upstairs to put on a pair of truly ancient trainers, and just happened to glance through the bedroom window as a car drew to a halt outside the house. It was the estate car she had last seen parked on the drive outside Cerne Farm, and there, getting out of it, was Julian.

'Blast!' she muttered to herself. What was he doing here? How much more pain could he possibly inflict on her? She cowered in the bedroom, trying to pretend she was not there, that she had gone to Timbuktu on business—anything, so long as he would go away. But he stood on the doorstep, ringing the bell loudly and imperatively, and she knew him well enough to be sure that he would not give up until he had whatever it was that he wanted.

'All right—I'm coming,' she shouted, and cast a horrified glance at herself as she passed the hall mirror. She *would* have to look like something the dustbin men had left behind, she thought wretchedly, and, whatever he had come to say to her, she did not want him to remember her like this. *It doesn't matter*, she told herself sternly. Just tell him to go away, and it will all be over.

She opened the door and there he was, tall, powerful, his frame filling her vision, crisp, shining hair, clean profile, that wry hollow appearing at the side of his mouth. Her one and only love. She faced him stonily, not knowing what to say that would make any sense, and yet not leave her defenceless.

'You took your time answering the doorbell,' he said coolly. 'Anyone would think you were surprised to see me here.'

She stood her ground, although he was too close for her to feel comfortable.

'I am,' she said. 'I really can't imagine what you are doing here.'

'Nor can I,' he said witheringly, 'except, let's say that I don't like it when someone makes a complete U-turn without any reasonable explanation. I stewed over it all day yesterday, and finally came to the conclusion that it simply wasn't good enough. Now, are you going to invite me in?'

'No, I most certainly am not. You might be used to people jumping around obeying your orders without question, but you can't play that game with me,' she said coldly.

'Oh, spare me all that old hat,' he said contemptuously. 'You are going to talk to me, as one human being to another, whether you like it or not.'

'I think not,' she stonewalled defiantly.

'I think so. Absolutely,' he said, with complete and utter certainty. 'If you won't ask me in, then I suggest we go for a walk.'

Frankie, hands firmly on her hips, said, 'I'm going nowhere with you, thank you very much!'

By now, Frankie's ever-curious next-door neighbour had appeared in her front garden, and was making a great play of cutting dead heads off roses. Across the street, two men were washing their cars, and Frankie was aware that her raised voice had attracted considerable attention, which could only increase as more and more people came out to have a look what was going on.

'Frankie,' Julian said with resolute authority, 'we are going to talk, because I am not leaving here until we have. So if you would prefer us to have this conversation on your doorstep, with the entire neighbourhood as an audience, that's fine by me. It might be a little embarrassing for all concerned, since there have been matters between us that should not be for public consumption, but if you can handle that, why should I demur?'

She glowered at him viciously, out-manoeuvred by this blatant blackmail which she did not question that he would carry out if necessary.

'Oh, very well,' she muttered angrily. 'But look at me—I was all set to clean out the shed! How can I go anywhere looking like this?'

'You'll do fine. We can walk on the Common. There's hardly anyone about there at this time on a Saturday morning.' He shepherded her firmly down the path, calling back laconically to the interested watchers, 'See you folks later.'

He was right. Two men passed them, walking dogs, and a miserable-faced jogger trudged along in the distance; otherwise they had this part of the Common to themselves.

'You can let go of my arm,' she said, tight-lipped. 'You don't scare me, and I'm not going to run away.'

'Oh, no?' he challenged, eyes like specks of agate. 'So why did you back out of coming down to Cerne Farm this weekend? Getting a little too hot for you, was it? Temperature more than you could cope with?'

She flushed with anger and humiliation.

'If you must know the truth, I didn't think I should be sleeping with you while you were negotiating a reconciliation with your ex-wife,' she said glacially. 'Nor would I have, had I known. But you didn't choose to tell me, did you?'

He stopped in his tracks and turned to face her.

'Do you think I planned what happened between us?' he demanded incredulously. 'Damn it, Frankie, it *just happened*, and surely you must realise that. You're not some dewy-eyed teenager who has to be ritually seduced!'

'Neither am I a quick tumble for someone who just wants to get his hand back in for the big match!' she flashed back at him, all the suppressed hurt and resentment of the last twenty-four hours flooding to the surface.

For a moment she saw an answering fury flicker in his eyes, and then he said disgustedly, 'You honestly don't understand, do you?'

'Understand what?' She hesitated for the first time in her headlong condemnation, struck by the strange desperation in his voice, by a powerful emotion he was genuinely trying to convey to her.

'That, almost from the first day we met, I have been struggling to keep my hands off you,' he said forcefully. 'I knew it wouldn't do, not at first, that I wasn't ready, and I wasn't good news for any woman. I didn't want that feeling, either, not while I still didn't feel straight in the head—which was probably why I was so rough on you. I sensed that you weren't exactly immune to me, either. Don't deny it.'

'All right—I was far from immune to you from the start!' she admitted. 'Does it give you some kind of kick to make me confess that I wanted you?'

'Frankie.' He placed a hand on each of her shoulders and looked down hard into her eyes. 'This is straight talking now. I had been married for over fifteen years, but I had never, ever experienced anything like the passion you and I shared last weekend. I swear it to you!'

He paused and she stood speechless, trembling slightly, knowing he had more to say, and not daring to interrupt for fear of stemming the flow.

'We married very young, Alison and I,' he said. 'We had known each other all our lives, and as I once told you, in a sense it was expected of us.' He shrugged a little. 'I always felt that passion was something of an inconvenience to her. She held it at bay, and I never quite broke through.'

'But you loved her,' Frankie said, frowning. She could not quite bring herself to use the present tense. 'Fifteen years is a long time.'

'Well, yes. Love is an imperfect art when you're young, but you don't question it. I had excitement enough and to spare in my expedition work, and of course, we had the children.' A short laugh. 'I would come back from somewhere rough and dangerous to this beautiful home, where I felt a bit like an extra who had wandered on to the wrong stage set by mistake. It wasn't quite real.'

From far beneath the pain and tension, on a deeper, subconscious level, where they understood one another very well, Frankie was aware of a surge of grim humour welling up. She knew all too well what he meant. Still, she could not let go of the one salient fact that kept leaping out at her, again and again, which he had not denied.

'You don't have to tell me all this, Julian, simply because you and I were attracted to one another,' she said tersely. 'It's all irrelevant, since it didn't inhibit you from asking her to come back to you.'

'You're wrong about that,' he informed her shortly. 'I didn't. That was her idea. At her suggestion, we had lunch together after I saw my solicitor, earlier this summer, and she started to put out feelers then.'

'The day you came to dinner at my house,' Frankie recalled all too well. 'No wonder you were in a good mood! Ah——' She broke free and began to walk quickly across the grass, but he caught her up and held her firmly this time, hands gripping her upper arms so tightly she could not escape again.

'It's true I was feeling good, but that was because I had begun to realise that I didn't really need Alison any more. Maybe her infidelity had floored me when I came home from Amazonia, more because of the precarious state I was in, but, that day, I knew I was all but over it. I told her there was nothing doing. I didn't want to be the occasional model husband in her ideal home, and I certainly didn't want to make love to her. I wanted to make love to a real woman. You.'

Frankie stared at him uncomprehendingly.

'But... are you trying to tell me you hadn't thought of a reconciliation?'

He released her arms, but there was no way she could have walked away then. Her eyes were fixed on his face, watching for the slightest flicker of regret or longing.

'I thought about it, yes,' he admitted openly and without hesitation. 'It seemed to me that we were not doing too well by our children, and that as parents maybe we should set aside our differences for their sakes. I didn't rule it out, not initially.'

'Not initially!' Frankie exploded. 'Karin told me that she spoke to her mother only the other day, that you and she had talked, and that you were getting together again.'

Julian frowned deeply, and dug his hands deep into his trouser pockets.

'So that's it!' he said, as one who had suddenly made sense of a puzzle. 'Alison had no right to confuse Karin by saying that to her, especially as it simply wasn't true. Yes, I talked to her, and I told her categorically that we were finished. She ranted and raved at me, then, going on about how I wasn't fit to have the children; how, after a short time in my care, Karin's life had been put at risk. But she never came to see how Karin was. She used them against me when she left me—perhaps it helped to justify her own guilt. It doesn't really matter any more. I know I could never live with her again, not for any reason. I knew that after last weekend . . . after the time I spent with you.'

She gasped, and the blood ran from her lower limbs, leaving her weak and shaken. She shook her head, wanting to understand properly what he was saying, but so afraid of being hurt more that she did not believe it.

'No, Julian—don't——' she faltered, and he took her hand to steady her.

'It's all right, Frankie,' he said. 'You have told me more than once that your life is fine just as it is, that you're not interested in marriage or in having children. I can see that you have a flourishing career and a nice home, so put it down to an inborn arrogance I can't quite shake off, that I thought I could persuade you to upset the apple cart and take a chance on me.'

In the middle of Clapham Common, with the August sun climbing high in the morning sky, and watched by three adolescent boys idly kicking a football, Frankie Somers, thirty years old, responsible adult and efficient editor, burst into tears and bawled like a helpless baby.

Julian put both arms around her and held her tenderly.

'Don't cry, my love,' he said gravely. 'The last thing I want to do is to make you unhappy. I only want what you want. If you say the word, I'll go away and leave you in peace. You have me at your mercy.'

She looked up tearfully, sniffed, and rubbed her eyes on her sleeve.

'I want *you*, you idiotic, short-sighted man!' she sobbed. 'I love you—I've loved you for ages! But I thought . . . I thought you still loved Alison, and I didn't want to risk losing what little of you I could have!'

Julian took a long, measuring look at her, as if he could scarcely believe the miracle he was hearing, and then, satisfied he was right, he glanced over his shoulder at the three youthful footballers, who were chuckling and nudging each other interestedly.

'Do us a favour,' he said pleasantly, but with such authority that their mouths fell open. 'Get lost, will you, there's good lads?'

They slunk off without question, and he wrapped Frankie more tightly in his arms, tasting her forehead and her damp eyelids with his lips, and finally finding her mouth. She clung to him fiercely, unable to get too close, offering him her love and her whole life in one kiss.

'I love you,' he said at last. 'I didn't know what love could be until I met you. Forget what I said before—there's no way I am going to let you go.' His smile melted her bones, made her body as light as air, and yet heavy with need. 'How do you feel about the hazards of commuting from Canford Tarrant?'

'I'll commute from Outer Mongolia for you, if necessary,' she said fervently. 'I'll take on your present family, and any more you might give me—which I seriously hope you will. I'll live with you, or I'll marry you, if that's what you want. Either way, I'll never leave you.'

He laughed, a low, appreciative chuckle.

'Frankie—my dearest girl—now *I'm* shocked!' he said lightly but beneath the levity she could feel a strong and passionate sincerity she knew would be hers as long as she lived. 'You will have a ring on your finger, and be very properly Mrs Julian Tarrant. And that, my love, is an order.'

'Yes, sir!' she said delightedly, and hand in hand they walked slowly back across the Common to break the news to the world.

Next Month's Romances

Each month you can choose from a wide variety of romance with Mills & Boon. Below are the new titles to look out for next month, why not ask either Mills & Boon Reader Service or your Newsagent to reserve you a copy of the titles you want to buy – just tick the titles you would like and either post to Reader Service or take it to any Newsagent and ask them to order your books.

Please save me the following titles: Please tick | ✓

Title	Author	
DANGEROUS ALLIANCE	*Helen Bianchin*	
INDECENT DECEPTION	*Lynne Graham*	
SAVAGE COURTSHIP	*Susan Napier*	
RELENTLESS FLAME	*Patricia Wilson*	
NOTHING CHANGES LOVE	*Jacqueline Baird*	
READY FOR ROMANCE	*Debbie Macomber*	
DETERMINED LADY	*Margaret Mayo*	
TEQUILA SUNRISE	*Anne Weale*	
A THORN IN PARADISE	*Cathy Williams*	
UNCHAINED DESTINIES	*Sara Wood*	
WORLDS APART	*Kay Thorpe*	
CAPTIVE IN EDEN	*Karen van der Zee*	
OLD DESIRES	*Liz Fielding*	
HEART OF THE JAGUAR	*Rebecca King*	
YESTERDAY'S VOWS	*Vanessa Grant*	
THE ALEXAKIS BRIDE	*Anne McAllister*	

If you would like to order these books in addition to your regular subscription from Mills & Boon Reader Service please send £1.90 per title to: Mills & Boon Reader Service, Freepost, P.O. Box 236, Croydon, Surrey, CR9 9EL, quote your Subscriber No:................................... (if applicable) and complete the name and address details below. Alternatively, these books are available from many local Newsagents including W H Smith, J Menzies, Martins and other paperback stockists from 11 November 1994.

Name:...

Address:...

....Post Code:.........................

To Retailer: If you would like to stock M&B books please contact your regular book/magazine wholesaler for details.

You may be mailed with offers from other reputable companies as a result of this application. If you would rather not take advantage of these opportunities please tick box. ☐